PROJECT TERRA
BITES BACK

BY LANDRY Q. WALKER

illustrated by Keith Zoo

Penguin Workshop
An Imprint of Penguin Random House

For Bee. Always—LQW

Mom & Dad, thanks for being great parents,
always believing in me, and always encouraging
me to keep drawing—KZ

PRELUDE

"It's over," Elara whispered to herself.

Clutched in her hand was her first-year graduation plaque—a small treasure symbolizing everything that the young girl had been through since arriving at the most prestigious terraforming school in the galaxy—the Seven Systems School of Terraforming Sciences and Arts.

Feeling the weight of the plaque in her hand, Elara looked out from the courtyard across the horizon. All around her first-year students milled about, cheering and laughing. The sun hung overhead and refracted light through the glass towers of the ancient and prestigious school. Despite all the difficulties Elara had endured since she first arrived on the planet Paragon to attend STS—her school's nickname—she had never grown tired of it.

Elara's train of thought was interrupted by a monstrous roar.

"We did it!" shouted the gigantic creature of living rock that was Elara's friend Knot. Knot swept the much smaller girl up in a huge bear hug.

"Gak!" answered Elara, desperate to not get squeezed. "Blarg!" she added as her skin turned purple from lack of oxygen.

"Oh," Knot said in her high-pitched, squeaky voice. "Right! You're made of super-soft, squishy meat parts! I almost forgot!"

With that, she released Elara from the hug of doom.

"S'okay . . . ," Elara gasped. "Good to . . . know you care . . ."

"I'm just so sad. Our first year is already over!" Knot snuffled a bit, which sounded like two rocks grinding against each other. "It was all so wonderful! I will miss every second of it!"

Elara rubbed the bruises on her arms. "Uh . . . except maybe all those times we almost died?"

"Pish!" Knot said with a wave. "On my planet, near-death experiences are celebrated! Why, when we swarm the villages during the height of the red moon—"

"We graduated!" a snobby-sounding voice screeched, interrupting whatever Knot was about to reveal of her home world. That was Sabik. He was surprisingly not awful, given that he constantly sounded like he thought he was the very best thing in the world—a byproduct of growing up on the wealthiest planet in the galaxy.

Sabik ran up the steps to the graduation platform, holding his own tiny plaque. Beezle was behind him, with the immobile sponge, Clare, strapped awkwardly to her back.

"Sabik speaks correctly," Beezle said in her usual happy-sounding manner. "We have marked the passage of our education with the proper ceremonial tokens. Our parental units will be most proud of the trinkets we have acquired on this day!"

Elara jumped up, feeling terribly wistful. "Come here, all of you!" she yelled, pulling out her personal comm system and switching to camera mode. "I need a picture to get me through the summer break!"

"Ah!" Beezle exclaimed happily. "Yes, the voices in my head say that we absolutely must record this moment!"

Knot wrapped her massive arms around the group—once again, way too tight. But Elara didn't care. These were the very best friends she had ever had. For a brief moment, though, she felt a pang of regret. There was one more person she was wishing she might see—the strange time-traveling Agent Tobiias Groob. He had helped her and her friends through so much, but as soon as he had repaired his time machine, he had vanished.

Elara shook her head, refusing to let anything make her sad right now. She pressed a button, and the comm snapped the photo, the flash temporarily blinding the laughing group.

Elara flipped the machine around, looking at the image on the screen. In the distance, a great bell gonged. The school year was over, and Elara knew it would feel like forever before she had a chance to return to the wonderful, beautiful, yet somewhat crazy campus of the Seven Systems School of Terraforming Sciences and Arts.

CHAPTER 001

Elara had been absolutely right. The summer moved slower than any summer ever had. A creeping and crawling thing that never wanted to go away. Not that Elara hadn't been busy. No . . . as soon as she had stepped off the shuttle onto the landing platform of her home world, Vega Antilles V, her family had consumed every waking minute of her day. Road trips across the thousand-mile grain fields to visit cousins in the east. Train rides through the forests of fruit trees to see more family down south. It had all been utterly and completely exhausting.

And to make it all worse, the current trajectory of her planet had made any communication with her friends impossible. They all resided much closer to the galactic capital than Elara did. All of them except Clare, anyway, who lived only one system over. But her world was a primitive swamp planet, and Clare never spoke, wrote, read, or communicated in any way that Elara had been able to perceive.

And so Elara found herself several weeks into the endless summer, sitting in her family living room, tapping away at the interstellar comm system for the billionth time. She was once again rewarded with the offline tone noises—a steady buzzing that filled the house. A sound Elara had heard so much that she had begun to dream about it.

And then suddenly, her moping was interrupted. "You spend way too much time on that thing."

It was her little brother, Danny. Days away from his tenth birthday, Danny was small for his age. He could easily still pass for seven years old.

Elara glared at her brother. "I might still get a signal . . ."

"Pff . . . ," he answered. "Not likely. They said on the news there was too much interference because of a nebula. In a couple of weeks—"

Elara threw a pillow at her brother. “A couple of weeks is forever!” she yelled. “And I’ll be back at school by then, anyway!”

“Right!” he said, throwing the pillow back. “So let’s go do something! Something fun!”

“I just want to go back to school!” she replied, pulling the pillow over her face. “I want to see my friends . . .”

Danny was persistent. “I know something else we can do . . . ,” he sang in a tempting tune. “Something you’d really, really, really like . . .”

Elara looked out from the pillow, her curiosity piqued despite her sour mood. “What?” she said cautiously. “What are you talking about?”

“Come on!” he said, the excitement rising in his voice. “I’ll show you!”

Before long, Elara found herself in one of the massive grain fields on her family’s farmland. She could hear the herd of distant gohrinios as the two-headed quadrupeds grazed nearby. It was dark, and the night was warm. There was nothing to see out here that Elara hadn’t seen thousands and thousands of times.

“Danny . . . ,” Elara complained, “there’s nothing here!”

“No . . . look!” He started to run deeper into the field. “Check it out!”

“Hey!” she yelled, running after her little brother. “Wait up!”

She caught up with her brother a few moments later. Danny was pointing to a bare patch of ground. Unusual in a field of grain, but not impossible. Then Elara did a double take. The ground wasn’t the same earthy, brown texture as the surrounding soil. Instead of rich dirt, a small three-inch-by-three-inch section of ground was sleek, smooth, and bluish white.

“What . . . is that?” Elara said, stammering.

“Ice!” Danny exclaimed proudly. “I read all of your homework and the books you brought home. I thought I’d try to make the ground colder. Y’know . . . terraforming!”

“Well . . .” Elara shrugged. “I mean, terraforming is more complicated than temperature regulation . . . but this is really impressive.” She poked at the icy patch. It was cold and slightly damp. “How did you establish the boundaries on the climate zones?”

“You mean why doesn’t the ice melt?” Danny asked, digging in the ground nearby and exposing some metallic objects. “I borrowed some field generators from the barn. The ones used to set up herd fences. Your books said that field generators are used to contain weather and stuff. So I figured it would work.”

“Yeah . . .” Elara nodded. “This is nice work, Danny.”

“I can’t seem to make it get any bigger, though,”

Danny said, kicking dirt back over the field generator. "I know you have to do important stuff like sit and stare at the comm system all night, but I was kind of hoping you could help me with this?"

Elara nodded and kneeled down to the ground. She dug a trench with her finger around the perimeter of the icy patch. "The ground here is really dry. Your ice sucks up a lot of moisture. Go get me a cup of water. If we're lucky, we can even make it snow a little."

Elara spent the rest of summer playing in the fields with her brother, teaching him about the mechanics of weather. With the comm system still down, she had nothing but time to help Danny improve his terraforming project. By the end, they had managed to make a six-foot patch of snow and ice in the middle of the field. Within that, the siblings built a tiny ice fortress and a snowman to guard against interlopers.

And then suddenly, all the weeks in the calendar were crossed off. The school break was over. Elara soon found herself packed and practically running out the door. She hated to leave her family, especially her brother. It all seemed so fast.

But it was time.

CHAPTER 002

Elara sat at the train station once again. Her family had dropped her off more than an hour ago and waited as long as they were able. But her parents had to get home and tend to the farm before sundown. And her brother had to prepare for his first year in the fifth grade—a big step for him. So she hugged everyone and smiled and told them all that she was ready for her next year at the Seven Systems Terraforming School of Sciences and Arts.

And technically, she was. She had all the books and equipment required for a year-two student. She had studied the curriculum guidelines that had been handed out at the end of the previous year. And though she wanted desperately to see all her friends again, now that the day was here, she was feeling . . . anxious.

Opening up her backpack, Elara removed a worn and battered copy of the school handbook, flipping through it casually. She had owned this particular copy ever since she first decided she wanted to pursue a career in terraforming. It was missing half the cover, and a milkshake had spilled on it at some point. But it was still readable. You could still make out the pictures of the school and the planet of Paragon. A shimmering campus of glass, wood, and water . . . translucent purple oceans . . . skies filled with jellies . . . air that smelled like cookies fresh in the oven . . . It was a magical place—one Elara had been desperate to see for herself last year.

But being cut off from daily communications with her classmates left Elara feeling out of the loop. Like it was her first year all over again. After all, her first year as a student had been . . . very weird. While most of her peers had learned how to shift atomic structures or build stable atmospheres, she had been busy trying to not get killed by remote-controlled robots and multi-tentacled spider squid kitten monsters. A mysterious time traveler and supposedly extinct alien race hellbent on destruction had also come into play. Overall, it had been a little bit stressful.

This year would be different, though, Elara swore silently to herself.

The sun was high in the sky overhead, and Elara felt the heat keenly. She still had headaches—an unfortunate side effect from swallowing Nebulina's terraforming marble—the only way to save Paragon and STS from destruction. The pain flared up occasionally, but physicians agreed this would pass in time.

Yup. This year would be different. She had friends to travel with, a school that was familiar, and a second chance to study in a normal, quiet environment without any nightmarish distractions.

When the shuttle finally arrived, she boarded it, found her seat, and settled in.

The shuttle was the same as Elara remembered it: a long, narrow, computer-controlled vehicle. There was a large open area with several empty seats, as well as private compartments for groups of four. Elara's planet was the first stop for this shuttle car, and Elara was alone. Dropping her backpack in a seat, Elara settled in inside a four-person cabin, saving the seats for her friends.

Her eyes grew heavy as the shuttle jumped into hyperspace. It would be a few hours before she reached another car of students.

Just a little nap, she decided.

Elara woke to the familiar sensation of the shuttle docking. She heard a hissing noise as oxygen flooded the hatch between her car and another vehicle. It was too early to have reached any of her friends' home planets, but still . . . it would be good to see another classmate. Maybe even make some new friends during the trip? Burying her anxiety and feeling a fresh wave of confidence, Elara pushed the button and stepped through the hatch into what she assumed would be another shuttle car.

It was not.

Instead, Elara found herself inside a giant hangar. The floor was a firm, rubberized surface, and the walls were stark white, gleaming and shiny. Several display screens were mounted high up, near the vaulted ceiling. Along one side, next to the hatch Elara had just stepped through, was a window. Outside the window, all Elara could see was the vastness of space.

"What . . . the . . . ?" Elara heard herself say.

Her confusion was interrupted by a noise. From

across the large room, a doorway slid open. "Hello . . . ?" Elara called out. "Who's there?" she asked.

"100100001010000," came a reply, speaking in a voice devoid of emotion. "0010010101," it continued.

"What?" Elara asked. Something was wrong. Very wrong. "Who are you?" she demanded as a figure emerged through the distant doorway.

The shadowy figure approaching Elara wasn't human. Nor was it humanoid. That wasn't alarming. There were multiple species in the Galactic Affiliation that were of non-humanoid descent, and all were considered peaceful.

But this wasn't even a non-humanoid, Elara realized as the form grew closer. It wasn't even a living creature. "A robot . . . ?" Elara whispered.

It wasn't like any robot Elara had ever seen—and she had seen many. Robots were limited to simple service droids, or mentally controlled machines used in construction and sports. But this robot was far more advanced than anything Elara had ever imagined.

"1001000101110010!" the robot said, more forcefully.

The robot had no face. Not really. Instead it had a screen, housed within a large rounded body of grayish-silver metal. The screen projected a pulsating green line that wobbled every time the robot spoke. The robot had several thick metal tendrils dangling from its frame that only just touched the floor.

The robot reached out with a tendril. Elara braced herself. She had no idea what was about to happen, but clearly it wasn't good.

"Oh," the robot said, suddenly speaking in a much friendlier voice. "My apologies. My vocal modulator was recently serviced, and I am afraid that I forgot to deactivate my binary machine language."

"Ah," Elara responded, thrown off guard. "You're . . . uh . . . not attacking me?"

The face of the robot flickered into a frown. "Of course not! My name is TN-G13. I am tasked with greeting all new arrivals to the school."

"But . . . ," Elara stammered. She glanced around at the white walls. The rubberized floor. The window into space. "We're in space. This isn't Paragon. This isn't the Seven Systems School . . ."

"Of course not," the robot said, a smile icon flickering on its screen. "The Seven Systems School of Terraforming Sciences and Arts is closed."

Elara felt the floor shift under her feet. She blinked uncontrollably. "Closed?" she whispered, confused.

"Yes," the robot said with a saccharine tone of politeness. "Welcome."

CHAPTER 003

Elara's head was still swimming as she followed the robot down the gleaming white corridor.

"The school . . . ," she asked. "STS is closed?"

"Again, yes," the robot answered. "This way. Orientation is just about to begin."

The robot gestured with one extended tendril. "Through here, please."

"But . . . ," Elara said, looking back at the robot as she stepped in through the door. "How . . . ? Why . . . ?"

The door slid closed with a *whoosh*. Elara felt coldly alone as she stared at the sterile white surface of the door. Frustrated, she reached up with a fist and punched it.

"What is going on?!" she said, emotion welling up in her voice.

The room descended to a hushed silence. Which was weird, because Elara hadn't realized until that moment that the room was occupied.

Already knowing what she would see, Elara slowly turned around. Yup. There it was. Everyone in school. Well, all the second-year students, anyway. Hundreds of them, all staring at Elara with their mouths silently agape, judging the young girl in only a way that twelve-year-old students can.

"Ahhh," Elara said, her cheeks burning with embarrassment.

The crowd of students should have been a comforting sight. But instead, it all added to Elara's confusion. Everyone was wearing identical jumpsuits, black with a green stripe down the center, all the way to the bottom of the pants, which flared at the ankle and ended in a pair of sleek-looking black boots. Even stranger, the crowd of students were lined up in perfect order, rows and rows of them. They were all facing a stage—the room appeared to be some kind of amphitheater.

Suddenly a familiar voice called out. Elara glanced back at the crowd and saw Beezle pushing her way out of formation to greet her. "Oh!" Beezle said, reaching Elara and grabbing her with a tight hug. "Hello, friend Elara! It has been so very long!"

With some reluctance, Elara pulled away from the comforting hug. "Yeah . . . Beezle. What is this? Where are we?"

Beezle tilted her head in a manner that Elara had come to understand indicated confusion. "Well . . . we are at school, correct? Why were you screaming, Elara? Were you discomforted by the transportation systems?"

"The what?" Elara sputtered, confused by Beezle's lack of alarm. "Beezle? What are you all talking about? This isn't—"

Elara heard a laugh from the back of the crowd. It was a voice she remembered all too well from her first day of school last year—rich-girl bully, Suue Damo'n.

"*Pff* . . . this is so typical!" Suue mocked, stepping forward. "Like you didn't hog enough attention last year with all your little stunts? You need to start the first day of school being a total drama queen?"

A general giggle went through the students.

"Wait," Elara said, brushing away Suue's taunts. "Just someone explain . . . why are we here?"

Suue rolled her eyes. "I know why we're here . . .

no one has any idea what *you're* doing here, though, that's for sure."

More snickers from the gathered students. Elara glanced around. She saw several familiar faces besides Beezle and Suue. Peter, Silent Dave, and the boy who called himself Scrubby were all standing behind Suue, as usual. She also saw Sabik—the small Suparian had apparently just arrived and was trying to push his way through the crowd with all four of his arms, very upset about something.

"Hey!" Sabik hissed at the crowd. "Commander X30r! He's coming! You all want detention?!"

The crowd dissipated quickly, and the students lined up in neat rows.

"Who's Commander X30r?" Elara asked. "Beezle . . . Sabik . . . what is going—"

"Oh no . . . ," Sabik whispered, his reddish face going pale. "Your uniform! Where's your uniform?!"

"What . . . ?" Elara suddenly realized she was the only student not wearing the black-and-green military-style uniform. "Why are you all dressed like that?"

Elara heard someone giggle. Tired of being laughed at, Elara turned her head to snap back. "Whoever that was—"

"ATTEN . . . TION!" a thick and commanding voice called out. "Students in ORDER!"

Beezle and Sabik pushed the disoriented Elara into the line. Elara strained her neck to see who the booming voice belonged to. She started to ask but noticed that everyone, from Suue and her minions to Sabik and Beezle, was standing still at attention.

A metal sound could be heard echoing through the large room. "Am I to understand that already, on our very first day of class, you students have fallen to chaos and disorder . . . ?" the loud voice continued. "Is that what's happening here?"

"NO, SIR!" shouted all of Elara's classmates in unison.

"Then explain to me why I heard yelling when I entered this chamber!" the voice bellowed once more. "Explain to me why . . ."

Elara blinked. The owner of the voice had reached her, and Elara could only guess that this was the aforementioned Commander X30r. Standing before her was another robot, this one even larger than TN-G13. Commander X30r was a floating, orb-shaped robot with a hollow side that housed a simple projected face. The robot's eyes and mouth were a series of moving dots and lines—all expressed in a digital display. The metal was painted to resemble a military uniform, decorated with multiple ribbons and gems. Elara imagined it meant something important, but she honestly had no idea.

Elara tried to stay hidden in the lineup, squishing between Beezle and a student she didn't recognize. But the robot instantly zeroed in on her. "You . . . ," the sentient machine said, "are out of uniform!"

"Yes!" Elara agreed, her frustration getting the better of her. "Apparently I am! But it would have been nice to know that I was supposed to be in a uniform!"

The robot's digital face displayed a scowl. "Are you claiming ignorance, student? We have made the dress code readily available in all school literature!"

"Look," Elara said, fishing her battered school handbook out of her backpack. "This is the only literature I have ever received! And there is nothing . . . at all about ANY of this in here!"

"Headmistress!" the robot roared after a moment. In response, a bluish light flashed in the center of the room. A semitransparent hologram of a humanoid appeared—female in design but otherwise nondescript.

"Yes, Commander X30r? How may I assist you today?"

"This student," X30r growled. "Who is she?"

A beam of light scanned Elara, causing her to flinch. "This young woman is Elara Adele Vaughn—second-year student. From the remote world of Vega Antilles V. Consequently . . ."

"Yes, yes . . . ," X30r said with a dismissive wave.

"She was outside of range of our training module. Thank you, Headmistress."

The hologram vanished. Elara could only guess that she had just seen some sort of computer simulation. There appeared to be no headmistress at all, more like a personal data assistant. She had seen them before, but never one so advanced.

"What's going on?" Elara asked again. "I mean . . . seriously. Why aren't we at Paragon?"

"Elara Adele Vaughn," the commander replied in a much more civilized voice. Shockingly, he offered a small bow as he spoke, his orb-like body dipping forward in a show of respect. "My apologies for the confusion. I am Commander X30r, the newly constructed headmaster of this educational facility. Your world was unfortunately outside communications range. An oversight on our part. But we will see that you are brought up to speed soon enough."

With that, a mechanical arm extended from the robot's hovering body. The commander tapped a button, and the wall on one side of the room slid back, revealing a massive window. All the students broke ranks in an effort to look, and a general chatter broke out. Through the windows they could see the stars, bright and shining in a way they never looked through the atmosphere of a planet. Several smaller ships could be seen, triangular fighter drones.

"Don't worry," the now-polite commander answered. "The security drones are here to ensure our safety as we travel throughout the galaxy, exploring education! For your safety is our number one priority!"

"You are a part of something new, Elara," the commander said as its face broadcast a smile. "You all are a part of a new, more practical educational experience. One that trains you—not just in science and art, but in survival."

"Welcome, cadets!" the robot intoned. "Your mission begins . . . now!"

CHAPTER 004

"The school was closed down?" Elara asked, still reeling from the information.

Beezle nodded solemnly. Elara felt herself grow cold, and it wasn't just because of the harsh and sterile spaceship she was walking in.

The commander had dismissed the students, and Elara quickly found herself ushered out of the hangar, down a series of hallways, through a dorm wing, into a cafeteria, and back out through the science labs. All the while her two friends tried to bring her up to speed on the many features of the ship. It was really an amazing spacecraft—filled with state-of-the-art classrooms, a vast library, a hydroponics bay providing freshly grown plants, and fully equipped science labs. The ship's interior seemed to be made of a white plastic-like material, and the engines of the massive vessel ran so smoothly, they were only vaguely noticeable as a slight hum.

They also passed several other faculty members—all robotic builds similar in construction to the commander. A whole teaching staff of floating orbs with digital faces and a variety of robotic limbs. Apparently, these automated beings were the new teachers of terraforming, fully programmed to exercise and promote educational services.

It was weird. It was overwhelming. And it was impossible, based on everything Elara knew about robotics. But according to Sabik, whose family was deeply involved in the production of technological goods, the robots had been on the assembly line for months, developed specifically by the newly appointed overseer of education to help shepherd the new line of galactic schoolships.

"I don't understand," Elara added, desperate for more information. "The STS . . . Paragon . . . it's been in place for centuries. It's a revered institution!"

Beezle shrugged. "After Headmistress Nebulina attempted to resurrect the evil Frillianth, the governing body of the Seven Systems determined that the public location of the school was too much of a risk."

"Yeah," Sabik added. "Everyone got real paranoid about conspirators after Nebulina flipped. They've been having all sorts of hearings and loyalty tests and stuff. It's been pretty intense. The president of the council even created a new department of the government. It's a Security and Science branch. Run by a guy called the Watchman of Education."

"And so now we have robot teachers?" Elara asked.

"It is true," Beezle said solemnly. "In addition to keeping the school mobile, the Galactic Council decided that students would be safer under the protection of dedicated AIs programmed to loyally serve the Affiliated Worlds."

Elara rubbed her forehead, feeling a headache burning deep behind her eyes. "I've . . . I've missed so much," she said. "All of this is because of the things that happened. The stuff we were involved with . . . ?"

"Yeah." Sabik nodded. "But no one really knows just how involved we were."

Beezle quickly agreed. "It seemed like it would be better not to share the details overly much. There is so much stress revolving around the Frillianth's return."

"Okay . . . yeah . . . ," Elara agreed. The previous year had been bad. But she had never imagined, not in a million years, that so much might change because of it. But despite how strange it all was, Elara's mind was laser-focused on one sad truth—the school of her dreams, the campus that had birthed the designs of thousands of terraformed worlds, was closed. Closed and replaced with . . . this.

"So now we have class on these spaceships?" she pressed, still hoping that she had somehow misunderstood.

"Schoolships," Sabik answered. "There's a small fleet of them. Each one is a self-contained mobile learning environment. We're stationed on board for the entire school year."

"It is quite a change!" Beezle said with her usual smile. "And it is unfortunate for you to find out this way. We have all been trained throughout the summer, thorough mandatory drill sessions ordered by the Watchman. You were supposed to receive instructional packets and a holo-instructional cyber summer course preparing you for our new reality."

" I get it, I guess," Elara said finally. "All that stuff last year was pretty bad. Still, this is a lot of change . . ."

"It's all new," Sabik admitted. "It all came in with

the new Watchman. He's supposed to be some kind of future tech wizard."

"It's much safer." Beezle smiled. "The teachers are specifically programmed to look out for our best interests, and they cannot be corrupted by outside forces like the Frils."

"Wait . . . ," Elara said, suddenly concerned. "Where's Knot? And Clare? They didn't get placed on another schoolship, did they?"

"I don't know." Sabik blinked. "Everything was kind of crazy after you showed up. I forgot to ask."

"We only just got here, shortly before you," Beezle added.

"Well . . . ," Elara said, frowning heavily. "Maybe we can ask now. Headmistress!"

A now-familiar bluish light flared up in the corridor. Elara stepped backward, trying to contain her surprise. Despite her effort, she hadn't really thought that she would be able to summon the computer hologram.

"Elara Adele Vaughn. How may I be of assistance?" the hologram chirped.

"Um . . . hi, Headmistress," Elara ventured, pushing back the uncertain tone in her voice. "Um . . . just so we're clear . . . what are you?"

"How nice of you to ask," the holographic projection buzzed. "I am an interface systems analytics automated processing projection, synchronized within a .00001 optimum frame-speak to meet the needs of all students assigned to this schoolship."

"Great." Sabik snorted. "I need pancakes."

The AI responded with a sudden laser scan of the Superian. "My scans suggest that you absolutely do not need pancakes," the AI intoned. "I would suggest a diet of fresh vegetables instead." Another scan, and the headmistress narrowed her eyes. "And exercise. Lots of it."

"Hey!" Sabik protested.

"So, you're here to help us, right?" Elara added.

The hologram flashed an empty smile. "I am here to aid the teachers and faculty of this schoolship in your education and to serve students by providing useful information as they adjust to their new learning environment." With a brief surge of blue light, the hologram added, "How may I be of assistance?"

Elara glanced at Sabik and Beezle. Sabik shrugged while Beezle stared expectantly back. "Okay . . . ," Elara responded, turning back to the hologram. "We're looking for our friends . . . they—"

"Ah. I understand," the hologram interrupted. "Researching list of known associates . . . Please hold!"

Sabik scowled. "She knows who we 'associate' with? That doesn't seem right."

"Well, she is a computer," Beezle countered. "I am quite sure she simply has access to our student records."

"Quite right!" added the headmistress hologram. "In fact, my data suggests that you are talking about Knot Wat and Clare Von Valentinus. Is this correct?"

Elara perked up. "That's them!

"Wait . . ." Sabik blinked. "Clare is a 'Von Valentinus'? Of THE 'Von Valentinuses'? She's, like, one of the richest beings in the galaxy!"

"Who cares!" Elara said with a quick glare at Sabik. "Where are they? We want to see them!"

"Hm . . ." The hologram frowned. "I'm so sorry, but one is a silicon-based life-form and the other is a methanogenic-based life-form. They are in quarantine and are not currently allowed visitors."

"Oh no!" Beezle said. "I do hope our friends are not suffering from some kind of ailment! I would find their sadness very difficult!"

"Relax, students," the hologram interrupted. "Your friends are perfectly healthy and are in safe hands."

"Wh-what?" Elara sputtered. "But then . . . why are they quarantined . . . ?"

"All non-carbon-based students are undergoing a temporary quarantine," the hologram said in a voice laden with sweetness, "while we bring all systems online. Do not fear. Your safety is paramount, and we are here to protect you."

The hologram winked one blank eye while giving a thumbs-up sign and an eager smile. Elara felt ill. "You mean . . . they're locked up? Because of who they are?"

"Only temporarily," the holographic headmistress assured. "For safety!"

"But . . . when will they be released?" Sabik asked the hologram.

"Very soon! As soon as our systems are ready and we can ensure all students will be safe!" the hologram said with a smile.

"But—"

"I hope I have been of assistance! Goodbye!"

And with that, the hologram shimmered away to nothingness, leaving the three friends to stare at the empty air where she had been.

The rest of the day passed without significant event. Elara and her friends discovered their dorm rooms—cold and sterile as the rest of the ship. While Elara's roommate hadn't checked in yet, Beezle was rooming with a multi-eyed Corranite girl named Sapple, and Sabik was with two heavily freckled, identical human twins who both went by the name of Milo Benjam. They all seemed nice enough, but Elara, Sabik, and Beezle were too preoccupied to socialize with strangers at the moment.

Instead, the three friends took refuge in Elara's empty dorm—a larger unit than the others, with two separate bedrooms and its own window looking out into the depths of space.

"So maybe it's a matter of environmental controls?" Sabik said. "Maybe they're just trying to get the life-support systems calibrated for multiple species?"

Elara snorted. "Yeah, I mean . . . sure. They can transport us across the galaxy somehow? But life-support systems aren't ready? How does that even make sense?"

"I don't know!" Sabik said glumly. "But there must be some reason. We just have to wait. I'm sure . . . I'm sure it will all be fine."

"It is all very unusual, I admit," Beezle offered hesitantly. "But there are a great many new policies in place since the Watchman was appointed to the board of education. It will take some getting used to."

Elara winced, not entirely comfortable with the idea. "Does the OverMind have any opinions about it?" she asked Beezle.

The OverMind was a sort of Arctuiaan hive mind that all of Beezle's species could access—one that transcended time and space. Elara wasn't quite sure how it all worked, though it really didn't matter if she understood. After all, the OverMind had warned them about the Frillianth attack last year.

But instead of shedding light on the issue, Beezle looked sad. "No. I must confess, the OverMind has been hard to access as of late. I believe that the ship's warp engines are causing a fluctuation in the matrix. I will try again when we land on a planet."

"Well . . . still . . . ," Elara mused. "Maybe you could try. Really try. It could be important."

"Or it could be nothing," Beezle replied. "Regardless, I have been trying. But as I said, it has been difficult."

"All right . . . well, we're on our own, I guess." Elara ran her fingers through her thick hair, pushing it out of her eyes. She couldn't help but think back to the same time last year . . . when she and her new friends were walking through the glass skywalk and into a massive and ancient living tree, polished smooth as marble. Everything then was so . . . magical. This . . . this was the opposite.

"Look," Elara said. "This whole thing. It's all a bit weird, right? Locking up non-carbon-based life-forms. There must be something we can do!"

"Oh no . . . ," Sabik said, rolling his eyes. "Let's not go down THAT road again!"

"What?" Elara pushed back. "What are you saying!"

"We can't get involved. Not again. Not this year. This is all too big—"

"But how can we not?" Elara responded, cutting the Suparian off. "I mean, all of this—"

Sabik threw all four of his arms up in exasperation. "Yeah! All of this. It all happened because of us, remember?" he snapped. "Because of Headmistress Nebulina and the Frils! It's been all over the news, and my Dad . . . he's on, like, three different government boards. He says everyone's freaked because the Frils attacked, and so . . . so everyone is worried! They're even preparing a fleet of ships—"

"What kind of ships?" Elara asked.

"The *warship* kind of ships!" Sabik responded.

Elara felt a burning sense of dread. "But . . . but there hasn't been a war in hundreds of years. And the Frils . . . they're stuck outside of time. They can't do anything!"

Beezle interrupted, her singsong voice strangely out of place in the conversation. "In fairness," the Arctuiaan girl whispered, "the Frillianth DID do something. They almost destroyed a world, and they almost returned."

"But we stopped them!" Elara shouted.

"And you gave them the technology they needed

to break free," Sabik said in a somber voice. "You were the one to solve the Impossible Equation. The terraforming bombs—"

"I didn't know that's what any of it was for!" Elara snapped back.

"I know!" Sabik said, standing up. "But still, we got involved and now the government is worried it might happen again."

The door leading to the outer corridor suddenly beeped. With a sigh, Elara got up to unlock it. The door slid open with a hiss and Elara came face-to-face with her new roommate.

"You have got to be kidding me," Suue Damo'n hissed from the hallway.

CHAPTER 005

Suue pushed her way past the speechless Elara. "Of all the people they could have put me with . . . ugh!" The mean girl dropped a heavy backpack down onto the floor. Seeing Sabik and Beezle, she rolled her eyes. "And you've already filled the place up with your little friends," she added. "How precious."

"Yeah, you're real special, too," Sabik answered with a glare. "Come on, Beezle. We should go set up our rooms."

"I suppose you are right," Beezle said with a glance at Elara. "Elara, will you be—"

"I'm fine, guys," Elara said to her friends as she gestured toward the new arrival. "I've had lots of practice ignoring her, don't worry."

Sabik and Beezle left, the door hissing shut behind them. "Well," Elara said after a long pause. "I guess we're going to have to somehow live together." Unable to keep the sarcasm out of her voice, she continued. "Yay."

"Whatever," Suue answered. "Don't start thinking we're about to become 'besties' or anything."

"Well, why don't you just put in for a transfer?" Elara jabbed back. "I mean, neither of us wants to live with each other!"

"Pff," Suue responded as she measured out the room. "This is the luxury suite. Though it hardly lives up to its name. My family paid for the best, I'm getting the best—even when it's a letdown. So, obviously you should be the one to ask to transfer. Go live with someone you don't make totally gag. Besides, there's no way a farm girl like you could afford a dorm room like this one."

"I have a scholarship . . . ," Elara murmured defensively. But despite her dislike of Suue, she had to admit that the pale-green-skinned mean girl made a good point. "Headmistress?" Elara asked the open air. "A quick question . . ."

The room glowed blue for a moment as the hologram manifested itself. "Elara Adele Vaughn," the now-familiar voice said. "How may I be of assistance?"

"Yeah . . . so hey," Elara said awkwardly, "how did I end up in this really nice room?"

"And how do I get rid of her as a roommate!" Suue yelled from across the room.

"This room was provided to you based on the record of your previous year," the hologram said politely. "Our calculations have determined that you are the most promising student at the school, and therefore have been afforded appropriate accommodations."

"Wait . . . WHAT?" Suue shouted, storming across the room. "She's the what now? How is that . . . no. . . . that is not a thing . . ."

The hologram smiled politely at Suue. "You are incorrect. It is a thing. Elara Adele Vaughn is the most promising student at the school."

Elara felt herself grow dizzy. Meanwhile, Suue was only getting more irritated. "No way . . . ," she grumbled.

"Yes way," the hologram responded.

"But then . . . then I'm also just as valuable? Otherwise I wouldn't be in this room, too!"

"Checking my records for . . . Suue Damo'n . . . ," the hologram spoke. "No. You are mistaken. You have not been designated as 'promising.' You are considered 'simply adequate' and have been paired in this room because computer simulations suggest that you and Elara are the best match for roommates."

"Okay . . . ," Elara said. "Now we know it must be broken because that is so not true."

Suue was reeling. "Simply . . . adequate . . ." was all she managed to mutter.

"I am not broken," the hologram said with a reassuring tone.

"How are she and I supposed to be a 'good fit'?! We hate each other!" Suue chimed in.

"Yes, that is on record," the hologram agreed. "And you are therefore statistically more likely to propel each other forward through a combination of frustrated rivalry and bitter self-determination. That is where true strength comes from, according to the database."

Elara felt her jaw drop. "What?! What about friendship? Trust and loyalty and love! I mean . . . why would you think two enemies would be good for each other?!"

"Mathematics!" the hologram said with a smile. "And math is always true!"

"Simply . . . adequate . . . ?" Suue said again.

"Suue . . . ," Elara said, turning to look at the girl. "Come on. Don't take it seriously. You know this is all ridiculous—"

"SIMPLY ADEQUATE?!" Suue yelled at Elara. And with that, she turned and stormed into one of the bedrooms, slapping the door control so fiercely it slid into place with a *slam*.

Elara winced. "Okay. Well, Headmistress . . . can't we just change rooms?"

"I'm sorry, Elara Adele Vaughn," the headmistress responded. "But room assignments are nonnegotiable. The computer simulation has determined what is best, and so it shall be."

"But—"

"I hope I have been of assistance! Goodbye!"

And just like before, the headmistress winked out of existence. With a sigh, Elara picked up her backpack and headed into the other bedroom. At least she was starting to get a sense of where she was and why she was there—no matter how strange and unappealing it might all be.

And maybe she wasn't being fair. Okay, so this new schoolship thing was different. And there was some weirdness going on with Knot and Clare—but surely that would be sorted out soon. It would probably all be fine. And by this time tomorrow, she and her friends would all be laughing and joking and having fun again.

But, ow. Her head . . .

Elara winced for a moment. The stress of the day had brought the side-effect headache back in full force. Elara punched her student ID code into the terminal next to the bed, bringing up the class schedule. "Six a.m. Formation and Inspection?" Elara whispered to herself. "Seven fifteen a.m. Drill and Discipline? What is this?"

Elara quickly scanned the rest of the schedule. It took a bit of doing, but she managed to identify some familiar courses. Geology. Atmospheric Reconstructions. Microbiology. Physics. They were all there. But so was Small Arms Training and Political Science. It was all so different.

Different isn't necessarily bad, Elara reminded herself again. *The teachers . . . the faculty . . . they're all professionals. They must know what they're doing. This will all make sense soon.*

At that moment, Elara's thoughts were interrupted by a blinding flash of light and a sound like two giant engines crashing against each other. It was disorienting, and yet . . . she had heard it before.

A portal in time and space had opened inside her dorm room. At the center of this portal stood a tall, lean, stern-looking human male with dark skin and grim eyes. He was holding a device in one hand that was covered in dials, around the size and shape of a small flashlight. The top of the device was spinning furiously.

It was Tobiias Groob. The time traveler from the future who had helped Elara and her friends stop the destruction of Paragon. Elara had no reason to think she would ever see him again. Yet here he stood, in the middle of her new dorm room.

"Everything is very bad!" Groob said before exploding into a million tiny dots of light that faded from existence as the portal of time and space collapsed.

The room was empty and normal once again. It was like Groob had never even appeared. Elara blinked. She was tired. She had a headache. It had been a long day. Maybe she had imagined it?

Something bumped her foot. A small metal cylindrical device. Elara bent down to grab it, gasping as she did so.

It was Groob's chrono-hopper. A portable time and space manipulation machine.

Elara felt her head pound as she rubbed her temples, examining the complicated wand-like device from the distant future. A faint whiff of smoke drifted from the machine, then all the blinking lights faded out. The machine felt cold.

Something was wrong. Something was really, very wrong.

CHAPTER 006

It was the first day of classes, and Elara had absolutely no idea what she should do. Groob didn't reappear. Nothing else out of the ordinary occurred. Only the chrono-hopper remained to convince Elara that everything she witnessed had really happened. The device was tucked securely in Elara's uniform pocket. And until Elara could figure out what to do with it, that's where it would stay.

Not that she had been able to find any time to think

about the situation. The first bell of the day had rung at five in the morning. All the other students were ready, jumping to action in uniform, while Elara dragged behind trying to keep up with her classmates. In this instance, that metaphor turned literal as the first activity of the day was a quick jog around the entire ship.

Exhausted, sweaty, and irritated by the end, the next morning ritual was a pledge to the Galactic Affiliation. It was like nothing Elara had ever heard before, though it seemed clear that most of the other students were familiar with the words—part of the training packages everyone had been sent over the summer.

> **To the Seven Systems, I declare, my loyalty and my promise,**
>
> **To uphold the laws that ensure peace, prosperity, and survival of all.**
>
> **I will trust.**
>
> **I will respect.**
>
> **I will obey.**
>
> **And because of this, I will be safe.**

As the students recited the pledge, massive monitors displayed a swirl of imagery. Images of the greatest cities of the Alliance, of the fields of the farm worlds and the mountain-size mines of resource-rich planets, all ending in a projection of a masked face wearing a dark hood. This was the new head of education—the mysterious figure known as the Watchman.

Elara couldn't help but stare at the image, wondering exactly who was behind that mask. There were several races in the galaxy that used masks and hoods to hide their features, either for spiritual reasons or for protection from the elements. Maybe he was one of those?

Regardless of his origin, the Watchman's message was clear: discipline, dedication, and most of all, loyalty to the Affiliated Worlds. These video messages rotated in and out of large screens in every room. And every now and again, the masked face of the Watchman would appear, with a fist raised in a salute and the bold letters *TRUST* emblazoned below.

The first actual class involving terraforming was held in the early morning. Each student was given a selection of spores and tasked with designing a soil that would support germination.

Elara's spores appeared to be a form of fungus—some kind of mushroom. Elara used the control panel on the biosphere she had been given to add more moisture to the soil—not too different from how she had helped Danny. But instead of making things colder, she increased the ratio of peat moss mulch in her soil mixture and added a layer of sandy soil under the richer dirt. Combined, these brought the temperature up by six degrees Celsius. Then she added some nutrients and shade, since mushrooms thrive in darkness.

The spores were bioengineered for accelerated growth. Elara's grew quickly, reaching their peak growth in about fifteen minutes. Boom. Instant mushrooms. At that point, the job shifted. Elara now had to treat the mushrooms as if they were a threat to the ecosystem and devise a way to halt their spread.

To do this, she brought the ambient light up, as well as the heat. With a quick sprinkle of lime and a thin layer of pea gravel, the extra moisture she had added vanished. The mushrooms died off just as quickly as they had grown.

Sabik was not having as easy of a time.

The Suparian had been tasked to grow, and then extinguish, Muddrakion tentacle root. This parasitic plant was found on worlds with no magnetic core, which normally protects the biosphere from solar radiation. Mutant plants like the tentacle root were a common, and dangerous, threat.

"You need some help, Sabik?" Elara asked.

Sabik's response was to turn a darker shade of blue and squeak out one sound. *"Glrk,"* he said. The

Suparian's feet were no longer touching the ground. The tentacles of the plant had wrapped around his throat and lifted him into the air.

The teacher of the class floated over—a smaller, pearly white robot called B3-09307i. The teacher had one delicate-looking arm that was affixed to its back, and the face display flickered a calm smile.

"Tsk. Those tentacle roots are certainly tenacious," the teacher intoned sweetly. "Hold very still, Sabik. Your dilemma is not lethal."

The teacher's arm unfolded, revealing a simple hypodermic needle attachment. With a quick move, the robot jabbed the needle into the tentacle root near Sabik's throat. The plant responded instantly, shaking at first, then relaxing. Slowly Sabik was lowered to the ground, visibly shaken.

"As you can all see," the teacher said with a smile, "even simple tasks can have grave consequences if you do not take careful steps to ensure your safety."

Elara shifted in her seat, feeling uncomfortable.

"Don't worry," B3-09307i said. "We are here to protect you."

Shortly after the first class of the day, Knot and Clare were finally allowed out of quarantine. For a very brief moment, Elara forgot about how weird it was to be going to school on a spaceship. The thing she had been waiting for all summer was finally happening. She was finally reuniting with all her friends.

"What were your conditions?" Beezle asked as she hugged Knot. "We were very concerned about your happiness!"

"I don't really want to talk about it," Knot grumbled before talking about it at length. "I mean . . . it wasn't bad. We were comfortable and everything. But it was so very frustrating." The Grix let out a deep stony sigh before continuing in her surprisingly melodic voice. "If the life support on these schoolships is really so unready, why aren't we just planet-side somewhere?"

"Is that why they have you wearing that collar?" Sabik asked, poking at the thick, semitransparent band around Knot's neck.

"Yes, this dreadful thing!" Knot shook her head. "It's to monitor my bio-signs to ensure I'm not having any negative reactions to the artificial environment. Tsk . . . really! I have been on seventeen different worlds—never a single problem. But now everyone's concerned!"

Clare was there, too. Knot had carried her in a backpack and placed her against a section of wall. The large rectangular yellow sponge also wore a collar, though on her it was more like a strap. After all, she had no actual neck or waist or limb or anything like that. Beezle was sitting next to Clare, whispering softly to the cube. Clare showed absolutely no sign that she was aware of anything. But she never really did.

Elara and her friends filtered into another classroom. This was to be a fairly basic class on planetary orbit shifting. Taught by a floating green-and-orange robot called CZ-833, the class was split into several teams, each one working on a holographic model of a planet. The goal was to alter the rotational axis to try to evoke a meteorological response, or rather, change the weather.

Elara and her friends formed a team, along with a friendly, dark-haired, gender-neutral Takkonite named Xavie that none of them had ever met.

"It is generally considered conducive," Beezle mused, "to shift a planetary axis by a minimal amount—no more than a degree or two."

"Yeah, but look." Sabik reached out and shifted the holographic image of the planet. "What if we did something way more dramatic like . . . this!" He stabbed at the hologram, adding a wobble to the rotation.

"Then everything on the planet dies," Knot said matter-of-factly.

"What if—" began Xavie.

"Hey . . . guys . . . I need to tell you something," Elara interrupted. "Groob appeared in my dorm last night."

Sabik groaned. "Oh no . . . not that guy again. We really don't need any more time travel drama."

"Our experiment . . . ?" Xavie tried to interject.

"It doesn't matter," Elara snapped. "We're talking about something big! Something important!"

"Honestly, Elara . . . ," Knot said as her mouth twisted into a frown, "can't it wait until after class?"

Elara glanced around. Their teacher was on the far end of the classroom. She shook her head. "It could be a while before we have this kind of privacy again. Look. Something is off. I mean . . . they closed STS!"

"We already talked about this . . . ," Sabik hissed. "It's obviously not good. But we're safe here. You have to admit, last year was all kinds of crazy. How many times did we almost die?!"

"Hunh?" said a very confused Xavie, who had never met, or even heard of Elara and her friends.

Knot shrugged. "Sabik is right, Elara. I don't like this very much. But there are good reasons for the changes. So . . . what are we supposed to do about it?"

"Something!" Elara hissed back.

"That is very vague," Beezle said.

"Elara . . . ," Knot added, placing a heavy stone hand

on the shoulder of her friend. "You have to admit, we've all been through a lot. And I only just got out of quarantine. Can't we just . . . take it easy? For a little bit?"

Elara pushed away Knot's hand. "Take it easy? A time traveler showed up in my dorm! He said . . . well, I think he was warning me!"

"What?" Xavie said, confused. "I don't understand this at all."

"You think it was a warning?" Sabik asked.

"It was unclear, okay?" Elara said, shooting a glare at her four-armed friend.

"So what's the problem?!" Sabik retorted. "What, Elara? We can't just start worrying without any good reason!"

"Besides," Knot added. "It would be nice to have a relaxing school year. One where we actually focus on our schoolwork."

"I, too, would like to learn things," Beezle added.

Elara narrowed her eyes. "But Groob . . . A time traveler doesn't just show up in someone's dorm room and then vanish because everything is okay! He even said everything is 'bad'! His words, not mine!"

"And so what?!" Sabik argued. "I mean . . . he's a time traveler! If there's a problem, he's way more equipped to deal with it than we are!"

Elara stood up, glaring in Sabik's face. "We have to help him!"

"With what?!" Sabik glared back.

Knot grabbed them both and forced the two friends apart. "Stop it. Both of you."

"You are being very bad friends," Beezle added.

"Sabik, we have to trust what Elara said. She's our friend and we have to," Knot said with a stern voice.

"Good!" Elara said with exasperation. "Finally. Now we need a plan—"

Knot turned toward Elara. "No," the Grix added, a rumble in her voice. "What we need to do is get our class work done. Then we need some rest. Then we can see if maybe—MAYBE—there is something we should be doing."

Elara sat back down, feeling sullen. There was a long pause. The tiny holographic planet continued to whirl in place, wobbling as it did thanks to Sabik's interference.

"I think . . . ," Xavie finally said carefully, ". . . that I should probably find a different study group."

Class ended. Elara's group was the last to finish, and by then their little planet looked horribly depressed, covered in ice, and fragmenting in several places.

"I just think you would feel better if you relaxed a little," Knot said to Elara as the group walked to their next class.

Elara crossed her arms and let out a snort. "*Pff!* I would love to relax! But something . . . something isn't right here! I can feel it!"

"Yes," Knot said, adjusting the uncomfortable collar around her neck. "It all sounds very serious. But life is often serious. We must not exhaust ourselves."

"I'm not exhausting myself!" Elara said, her chin stuck out defiantly.

"Yeah," Sabik said, glowering at Elara, "but you're not the only one here."

Elara narrowed her eyes, pulled her books up to her chest, and walked past her friends and down the ship's corridor to the next class.

CHAPTER 007

The next couple of days went by slowly. Elara was still angry with her friends, and not knowing how to handle that anger, she decided to ignore it.

The routine of the schoolship wasn't comfortable, but you did know exactly what to expect every day. It irritated Elara that she was getting used to the schedule. She had never been super good with early mornings, and these felt super early.

Elara mentally flipped through the routine. Morning

exercise jogging through the corridors, then showers, then breakfast.

Classes added a little variation, only because there was always something different to learn. But even then, the schedule was strict.

Hunched over a round table in one of the circular classrooms near the center of the ship, Elara flipped through her homework for the day. She propped her face up with her hand, elbow resting on the table. The subject was very, very boring.

She was sitting with both Milos, who had proven friendly enough in the absence of Elara's usual friends. *It's a good thing*, she told herself. She should branch out. Get to know other students. Sure.

Elara told herself this a lot, hoping she would eventually believe it.

Across the room, Elara could see her friends at their worktable. They were all focused on their studies, and they even had Clare with them. The sponge was an inanimate life-form from Thui Prime who couldn't move or speak, and even she looked like she was having more fun than Elara.

Elara rubbed the bridge of her nose. She was stressed and worried and scared . . .

. . . and now she was lonely.

It was a hard thing to admit. Maybe she shouldn't

have pushed so hard with her friends. And maybe she shouldn't have stormed off like she had. It was just . . .

Elara sighed. Things were different, but that didn't automatically make things bad. But . . . Groob's visit was a bit of an enigma. She couldn't just ignore his strange message . . .

"Article 0527.71," one of the Milos said to his brother, derailing Elara's train of thought.

"Yeah . . . I got that one," Elara heard the second Milo answer. "Non-carbon-based life-form ID Registration Provision . . ."

"What about the 'Demarcation Rezoning Initiative'?" the first Milo asked, making a note as he spoke.

Elara pushed up from her table and walked across the classroom. If her friends didn't want to get involved, it didn't mean *she* couldn't investigate. Something about this whole situation was off.

And she was going to find out why.

The school library was a large, windowless room located in the bottom of the ship. There were multiple computer stations scattered throughout and single-person cubicles that allowed a small degree of privacy. The rest of the space was filled with large shelves overflowing with data disk binders. No physical books appeared to be present on the ship.

Elara scanned rapidly through data files, all recent news pieces on the last several months of galactic politics. She programmed a set of search parameters into the library mainframe: anything relating to the "Seven Systems School" and the mysterious "Watchman" who had come to power so quickly.

"Nebulina = Traitor," one headline read. "The Return of the Frils," another reported. "Corruption in Our Schools! Are Our Children Safe?"

Every article read the same. They all spoke of the risks and dangers facing students, with parent groups speaking out against the lax security of the Affiliated Worlds' premiere terraforming school.

Elara shook her head. "But no one was hurt. We saved the planet. We stopped the Frils," she muttered. She flipped through more articles. The Watchman had shown up just after the thwarted attack on the school, and run for a Council seat in a special overnight election. That, by itself, was unprecedented. No one seemed to know anything about him or where he came from. From what Elara could understand, he stood for strong security and had promised to ensure that nothing would threaten galactic peace ever again.

Elara flipped through pictures. There might not have

been much in the way of news, but there were tons of photographs. The Watchman made his presence very public, holding rallies and making speeches on all the core worlds. He had become a familiar face at high-end political functions, even taking meetings with the president of the Seven Systems—the highest-ranking politician in the known galaxy.

Which was weird.

Elara rubbed her eyes. She had been looking through photos for hours. Each one the same. A cloaked figure in a mask. Only his eyes could be seen. Long black robes, almost covering his arms. He could be seen reading from books and slamming his fist down on podiums. But nothing that gave any indication of his identity, let alone his species.

Elara stopped flickering through the photos as her eyes went wide. She could barely see it. One photo. Just one shot taken during a meeting of the council, and most of it was obscured, hidden in the depths of the Watchman's hand.

A device. An impossible device that no one could possibly possess. Except . . .

Elara reached into her pocket and pulled out the chrono-hopper. It was still inactive, and Elara had barely begun to understand how she might power it back on. But there it was.

She looked back at the photo, zooming in on the Watchman's hand as closely as the screen would allow. It was unmistakable.

The Watchman was holding a chrono-hopper identical to the one in Elara's pocket.

The mysterious stranger that had closed down the Seven Systems School of Terraforming Sciences and Arts . . . was a time traveler.

It was late at night when Elara sent the messages, and even later when her friends finally showed up. She was sitting in the common room of the dorms, the lights off so as not to attract any attention. Beezle was the first to arrive, but Knot and Sabik were close enough behind.

"Okay . . . ," Knot grumbled. "This better be important. I get super grumpy when I don't get my beauty sleep, you know that."

"It is quite true," Beezle said, nodding in a deep affirmative. "I have witnessed this phenomenon. If unrested, Knot becomes quite cross and sometimes doesn't even fully enjoy her morning muffins."

"I was actually trying to suggest that I would get angry," Knot said, rolling her eyes. "Like 'rarrr' kind of angry, you know?"

"Oh," Beezle said, still smiling. "I meant to say she becomes quite fierce. All should tremble at her fury, for she is rage incarnate."

"Now you're overselling it," Knot said, shaking her head.

"Can we just get to the point?" Sabik said, yawning. "Elara . . . what is this all about?"

Elara sat in a chair in the shadows, slowly turning around with what she hoped was tremendous dramatic effect. "None of you believed me . . . ," she said, her voice a hushed whisper. "I told you something was really wrong . . . and now I have it."

"You have what?" Sabik asked.

"Proof!" Elara exclaimed, pulling a printout of the photo of the Watchman from her pocket. "I know why everything is so weird! It's because of this!"

"Ah!" Beezle said, taking the piece of paper from Elara and studying the back side of it with intensity. "I see! Truly, blank paper is our enemy! Together, we will crush it and all can be right once more!"

"No . . . ," Elara said, shaking her head. "Not that side. Beezle . . . turn the paper over."

"Ohhhh," Beezle said, looking at the other side. "You are correct. There is much more to look at on this side."

"But what is it?" Sabik asked. "I mean . . ." He glanced

over at the piece of paper. "So it's the Watchman? What about him?"

"Look at what he's holding!" Elara pointed.

Knot took the paper and studied it hard. Finally, she glanced up at Elara, confusion on her face. "A . . . pen?"

"No!" Elara whispered back intensely. "Look . . . it's a chrono-hopper, just like Groob's!"

"Oh," Sabik said, taking the paper back from Knot. "Okay . . . yeah . . . I can kind of see that."

"What do you mean, 'kind of'? It's identical!" Elara pulled Groob's chrono-hopper from her pocket. "See! Compare it!"

"Yes . . . ," Beezle agreed, yawning. "Those are indeed similar things. Okay. Now may we return to slumber?"

"But this means . . . a time traveler has taken control of everything! He's the one who shut down STS!"

"To protect us. To keep us safe," Sabik answered back. "We've gone over this."

Elara felt her confidence slipping away. "But he's a time traveler! And Groob said he was bad! Don't we have to stop him?!"

"I don't get it." Sabik shrugged. "So . . . a time traveler saved us last year, and now this time traveler is doing what? Protecting us?"

"Assuming he even is a time traveler!" Knot grumbled.

"Knot makes a very good point, Elara. He may simply have the same device. You have one, too, and you are not a time traveler. Maybe Groob gave him this. Maybe he is part of what is keeping us safe?"

"But at what cost?" Elara snapped. "Maybe . . . I mean, maybe we're safer here? But the Seven Systems Terraforming school . . . it was about making art! And building homes for people and transforming planets so crops would grow and ending famine! Everything we're learning now is about the military. And war. And everything that the STS wasn't! How can you be okay with that?!"

There was a long silence. Finally, Sabik shrugged.

"Because we're just a bunch of kids, Elara," he said. Then he turned and walked away. Knot grumbled and followed after. Finally, Beezle looked up at Elara, a sadness in her eyes. "I am sorry, Elara. But . . ."

Finally, Beezle shrugged. And she walked away to return to her dorm room.

Elara was alone. Still.

CHAPTER 008

Days passed. Wake up. Run through the halls. Eat breakfast. Attend classes. Wake up. Run through the halls. Eat breakfast. Attend classes. Wake up. Run through the halls. Eat breakfast. Attend classes. And at the end of every day, Elara would go back to her dorm room, ignore the glares from Suue, and try to figure out what she could possibly do to change how horrible everything had become.

For the most part, Elara didn't see her friends. When

she did cross paths with them, only Beezle was close to friendly. But it was hard to tell if that meant anything. Beezle's default personality was happy. Even when she was mad, she usually seemed happy.

A bell rang. It was the middle of the day, and Elara followed the corridor to her next class—Interstellar Botany. Once there, a yellow, four-armed robot informed the students that they would be experimenting with the effects of radiation on plant life.

"In front of each of you is a cube," hissed the masculine voice of the robot. "Inside each cube is a single plant, the most ferocious weed in the known galaxy—the *volubilis taraxacum*. Your assignment is to experiment with radioactive energies and catalog the effects of each form of radiation. Begin!"

Elara picked up her cube and pressed a button. It turned yellow. No effect. She pressed it again. It turned gray, and the plant started to grow. Elara quickly pressed the button back to yellow and wrote down what had happened.

Suue sat nearby, smiling smugly. The plant in her cube looked like it had transformed into something else altogether. Past her, Elara could see her friends, all sitting together, focused on their experiments.

Feeling dejected, Elara pushed the cube. Inside, a

single plant wilted in reaction to the radiation. Elara pushed it again, and the interior colors shifted from green to pink. The plant perked back up again but started changing colors.

Herbology and radiation was an important class. One that Elara should have been more invested in. She loved developing strains of plants that could easily adapt to survive on hostile planets. Plant life was the cleanest method of converting toxic atmospheres into breathable ones. They acted like air purifiers—the earliest and most reliable natural form of terraforming.

But Elara was distracted. She watched her friends and she felt . . . guilty. Last year, bad thing after bad thing happened. Everything was weird now, yeah. But things did seem safer. Why couldn't she just accept that?

That night, Elara felt particularly miserable. Her head was hurting more than ever, and nothing seemed to help. Lying in bed, she held the chrono-hopper in her hand, pressing at the various buttons, trying to activate the device in some way. To make it do . . . something. Anything.

And like every other night, no result.

Elara put the device back in her uniform pocket. She picked up the photograph of the Watchman and then sighed, crumpling the paper into a ball and throwing it across the room toward the trash can. The news all said the same thing: peace, prosperity, and economic equality for everyone. They were calling it the dawn of a new golden age. And here she was worrying because things weren't the same. Maybe the Watchman was a time traveler. So what? He was making things better.

Elara turned her light off, rubbing her forehead. First chance she got tomorrow, she would apologize to her friends for overreacting.

Hopefully by then her headache would be gone, too.

Elara woke up before the alarm—though it was way too early for anyone to be awake. She sat up, stretched, and yawned. She felt better. Maybe it was because she had finally decided that everything was okay.

She opened her eyes. Then she closed them again. Then opened one more time, hoping to see something different from what she had just seen. But no. No matter how many times she opened and closed her eyes, nothing changed.

Her room was filled with plants. Not potted plants, either. Somehow, overnight, living plants had grown out of the floor and wall and ceiling of her dorm room.

Elara rubbed her temples. Things were back to being weird.

The morning ritual again. A jog. Then the pledge. The giant screen with the masked Watchman telling everyone to trust. Then class—a particularly boring lesson on soil transformation. Finally, a bell rang, and the students all began filing out of class. But instead of continuing to their next course, they were stopped by Commander X30r and the headmistress hologram in the hallway.

"Congratulations, class," the commander robot barked loudly. "I have been watching you carefully, ensuring that you all were fit and ready to move on to the second stage of your acclimation! I'm proud to say that you have all shown the skills required to move on to our more advanced curriculum."

The teacher extended the long metal tendrils that hung from its frame, elevating above the crowd in a looming and menacing manner.

"Each one of your uniforms has an ID badge attached to the chest," the headmistress said, smiling. "If your badge blinks orange, please follow me. If your badge flashes blue, please follow the commander."

Elara looked down. Her badge flashed orange. Her friends' badges all flashed blue. "Hey!" Elara called to Knot as her group of friends started to file away. "Knot . . . I need to talk to you—"

"I'm sorry, Elara . . . ," Knot said, shaking her head. "I don't have the energy to fight right now."

"I don't want to fight!" Elara said. "I just . . . I just want to talk! Something really crazy has happened!"

"Well . . ." Knot looked around, seeing her group start to disappear down the hall. The light flickered, and Knot shrugged. "I can't talk. Not right now. Sorry."

With that, the large Grix turned away, her heavy footsteps echoing down the hall.

The headmistress blinked into existence where the Grix had stood a moment earlier. "Elara Adele Vaughn!" she said. "Please come along . . . mustn't dawdle."

"Fine," Elara said as she turned to follow the rest of her group.

Elara and a dozen other students were led into a large and empty white room. The walls were covered with ceramic tiles with lights built into each one. None of Elara's friends had been put in this group, and that made the young girl uneasy. Even if they were fighting right now . . . she felt better with them around. Instead . . .

"Why can't I ever get away from you?" Suue said, irritated to be anywhere near Elara.

"Feel free to leave," Elara said, glaring. Then, thinking better of it, she turned back to Suue. "Hey . . . does any of this seem right to you?"

"You're talking to me," Suue snipped. "So . . . no."

"No, seriously. The schoolships. All these changes . . . STS closing . . . ," Elara pushed. "Does any of this seem normal to you?"

Suue rolled her eyes dismissively. But rather than say something nasty, she shrugged. "I mean . . . ," she said, her voice hesitant. "Yeah. I guess it's all pretty weird."

Elara looked around. "Dave? Scrubby? They're not here. Have you talked to them about any of this? Do they think it's weird?"

Suue looked even more uncomfortable. With a heavy sigh, she finally spoke. "They don't."

Elara felt herself growing sick. She saw another girl she knew—Sapple, the Corranite who was Beezle's roommate. "Hey . . . Sapple? Right? It's not just us who think everything going on is weird, right?"

"No . . . ," Sapple said, looking a little scared. She was smaller than most of the students but still spoke firmly. "This is definitely not normal."

Elara glanced around, looking for a control panel to open the door. She couldn't find one. Locked. Trapped. Just a room filled with giant screens . . .

And suddenly it all made sense.

"Hey, everyone!" she yelled. "Raise your hand if you weren't part of the summer training program. Were any of you taught the pledge before you came here? I'm not the only one, right?"

A Suparian Elara didn't know raised a hand. "I was on vacation with my family. We knew about the changes, but I wasn't home to practice . . ."

A Deltaainian named Gunnir whispered shyly, "My family practices a spiritual cleansing during the summer months. We were forbidden outside contact . . ."

A Tharndarian nodded in agreement. A catlike Rakeesta called Mystie hissed an affirmative. A Jovvoon was on a planet similarly out of reach as Vega Antilles V. One by one, every student raised their hand. None had been a part of the rigorous training sessions. None had been watching and studying the pledge videos or reciting the newly adopted Alliance oath.

Elara glanced at Suue, curious. "What about you?" she asked the mean girl. "You live right in the galactic hub, right? Did you not get the package?"

Suue shrugged and looked a little embarrassed. "It just looked really boring, okay? I skipped it. No big deal."

Suddenly every light in the room flared on, flashing over and over again. Elara felt like she was going to be sick. She wasn't the only one. Several students fell to their knees.

A blue flash of light filled the already brilliantly illuminated room.

"Hello, students!" the holographic headmistress said. "We are here to help you! And over the course of the last several weeks, all of you have been identified as being a developmental step behind your classmates! To aid your transition, the Hypnoticon Broadcaster emissions in this room will wash away any troubles you might be feeling!"

Elara gasped. She heard another student let out a desperate cry.

"Don't worry!" the headmistress continued. "Your well-being is paramount! After treatment, you'll no longer worry or fret. And you won't question anymore. Instead, you will trust, respect, and obey. And because of this, you WILL BE SAFE!"

In the distance, Elara heard the pledge, over and over again.

I will trust.

I will respect.

I will obey.

And because of this, I will be safe.

The lights intensified. Elara felt sick. She stumbled to her knees. Her eyes closed.

I will trust.

I will respect.

I will obey.

And because of this, I will be safe.

Her head was pounding. Her vision swam. She felt . . . hot. Burning hot. And all the while, the pledge was growing louder.

I will trust.

I will respect.

I will obey.

And because of this, I will be safe.

Everything was swimming. Elara managed to open her eyes. The masked face of the Watchman filled the massive monitor hanging overhead. She heard voices. Not just the recorded pledge, but her classmates, all cheering along to the mantra, repeating it over and over.

I will trust.

I will respect.

I will obey.

And because of this, I will be safe.

And then it all stopped. The lights returned to normal. Elara staggered, rubbing her temples. Her headache subsided. Her vision returned to normal.

"Ugh . . . ," Elara said to herself. She looked around the bright white room. All the other students were standing still. It was . . . eerie. "Suue . . . ," Elara whispered to the mean girl. "Hey . . . you okay?"

Suue didn't answer—not a mean quip or a sneer or anything. For that matter, Suue didn't move. Suue didn't even blink. No one moved. Not even a little bit. Elara then noticed that every student was standing in perfect attention, lined up in exact rows. With a sudden sense of dread, Elara became concerned that she would stand out. She shifted her body so that she was in sync with all the other students.

The hologram headmistress floated around the room, casually examining the students one by one. "Excellent. This is so much better. So much more orderly, and . . . safe." The hologram paused a moment, staring at Elara. Her holographic smile faltered just a bit. Elara refused to glance. She refused to blink. But she couldn't stop the single bead of sweat from escaping down her forehead.

Luckily, the headmistress moved on without having noticed, and Elara relaxed internally. Her mind raced. She had been worried before. Now she was terrified.

"Okay then, students, I am so glad we had this little chat! From this point on, you should all find yourself far more comfortable in your new educational environment! No more pestering doubts and fears . . . no more curious and dangerous questions. From now on . . . you will all trust, respect, obey, and be safe!"

The students all opened their mouths and once again, let loose the pledge. Elara had just enough wherewithal to join them.

I will trust.

I will respect.

I will obey.

And because of this, I will be safe!

And then, single file, they all walked out of the room, ready to rejoin their classmates and take part in a healthy education. One that involved military strategy over science. Weaponized experiments over lifesaving technology. All without anyone questioning anything, ever.

The entire schoolship was a prison. A mind-controlling prison. And Elara was the only one not under its spell.

CHAPTER 009

All Elara could do was blend in. And if she was going to blend in—and more importantly, find a way to help her friends break the weird mind-control spell they didn't know they were under—she needed to act normal and do normal things. That meant apologizing to everyone.

The third class of the day was an open experiment. Students were to spend an hour creating bacterial strains that could change the concentrations of minerals in ocean water.

"Hey, guys . . . ," Elara said, approaching her friends as they injected a solution into the tank of water. The water changed color rapidly, developing a rainbow sheen. A sign that the bacteria was thriving. "Um . . . I just wanted to see if you wanted any help?"

Beezle smiled warmly, but Sabik and Knot looked suspicious. Clare was there, too. She was leaning against a desk, doing nothing.

"You're not trying to convince us everything is awful again, are you?" Sabik asked pointedly.

"No!" Elara answered. "I . . . Look, I'm sorry. This has all been hard for me. I wasn't prepared. Not like you all were. And with Groob showing up that night and then vanishing . . ." Elara pasted on her most sincere fake smile. "I guess I just got paranoid. And I took it out on all of you and pushed you when I should have been listening."

Elara felt her head start to hurt and her eyes twitch but refused to let any of it show. "I'm sorry," she said. "Can we just get a do-over on the school year?"

Knot stared at Elara for a minute, then broke out in a large smile, exposing her pointed, granitelike fangs. "Of course, sweetie! Come here . . ."

With that, Knot encircled all of them in one giant hug, squeezing just a little too hard, like always. Elara smiled, taking momentary comfort in the embrace. She closed her eyes for just a second and pretended everything was normal.

The rest of the day went smoothly. Elara didn't talk about Groob. She didn't talk about the shutdown of the Seven Systems School on Paragon. She didn't talk about the weird military uniforms or the creepy robot teachers or the masked Watchman. She didn't even mention the fact that she had woken up a few days earlier to a room filled with living, growing plants.

All she did was pretend everything was normal. And if you ignored the lack of curiosity about all the strange things going on, her friends seemed perfectly normal, too. They were still the same, just fully trusting in the new system.

They were still themselves.

"Which means I can still help them," Elara whispered to herself as she joined the formation of students marching down the hallway toward their next class. Atomic Compression Theory was a new course and took place in a laboratory positioned somewhere near the center of the ship. Most rooms located in the ship's inner chambers had slightly curved walls and harsh, white artificial light.

That is not what the students encountered when they entered the classroom. Inside, the room was filled with a bright and warm yellow light that felt like sunshine. There were green plants growing from the rich black soil that covered the floor and grew up along the walls. The entire far wall of the room was an open plexi-steel window. But this window did not look out into space. Instead, it looked onto the energy core of the ship: a luminous nuclear reaction, contained within a transparent sphere that sat at the heart of the vessel.

"It's amazing . . . ," Elara heard one of her classmates whisper.

"Beautiful," another said.

"Amazing," came the voice of a third.

Beezle's reaction was slightly different. The pale-blue-skinned girl made a slight clucking sound with her tongue and tilted her head sideways thoughtfully. "Oh," she said, to no one in particular. "Oh," she added, which did not help Elara understand what she meant.

"Don't you see?" Beezle finally asked, a tinge of excitement in her voice. "That sphere of energy—we invented that! Remember? By accident, last year in our Atomic Bioengineering class. The experiment that led to us being sent to the headmistress?"

Elara looked again through the window at the massive energy sphere. To the naked eye, it appeared to be built off the same principal—a continuous nuclear reaction folding over itself infinitely. It could serve as a power source for years and years . . .

"Hunh," she finally said in response. "I guess it's basically the same—just much larger. Weird, though. That kind of technology was supposed to have been outlawed. We made ours by accident—"

Sabik had drifted over to Elara and Beezle. "Eh. Things change. We didn't used to have spaceships—thousands and thousands of years ago, anyway. Now we go to school on one. That's progress."

Elara could only mutter under her breath, "That's a word for it, I guess."

Any further speculation of the energy sphere was cut short when Knot ran up to the group, her heavy stone feet reverberating through the ship.

"They have TINY kittens!" Knot said, her entire mountainous body shaking with glee.

"Like, little baby ones?" Sabik asked, not nearly as excited about kittens as Knot was. If Sabik hadn't already proven himself to be a decent being, that might have pushed Elara over the edge. No reasonable person did *not* get excited about kittens.

Knot looked down at the Suparian disdainfully. "No. I said tiny, and I meant tiny. See?"

With that last word, Knot carefully unfolded her hands and revealed the fluffiest, tiniest kitten that could have ever possibly existed—no more than one inch in length, including the tail. "Its name," Knot said in a grave voice, "is Mister Floofyface."

"It's . . . it's so adorable!" Elara blurted out, taking the kitten from Knot.

"Elara!" Beezle said with rising excitement. "Come look! There are many more kittens! We should all select one before they are claimed!"

There was no need to worry. The large, transparent container held more than enough miniature kittens for everyone.

Soon Elara, Beezle, Sabik, and Knot all had kittens—as did every other student in attendance. Even mean girl Suue had one that she was playing with, lying on her back and letting the super-tiny kitten jump up and down on the tip of her nose.

For a moment, the school didn't feel terribly oppressive and weirdly militaristic. For a moment, it was fun.

Then the joyful laughter and sound of tiny meows were interrupted by a hissing sound. A portal in the ceiling opened up, and within a few seconds a teacher-bot floated down. This teacher's metal frame was painted to resemble the student uniforms and had four heavily articulated claw arms protruding from its back.

"Hello, students," the female-sounding robot said in a pleasant voice. "I am Teacher G-33n. My role is to educate you on the exciting new developments our Science Council has made in the field of atomic reconstruction—specifically, the miniaturization of organic life-forms."

One student—a multi-horned Bloaraxian—raised his hand and asked a hopeful question. "So . . . so are we supposed to raise these? Do we get to keep one?"

The robot gave a small electronic laugh. "Keep?" she said, her face display reflecting amusement. "Oh no. These are laboratory animals—nothing more! We will start our experiment by creating biospheres to contain these creatures."

Another student interrupted. "But these are just . . . kittens."

The teacher's expression dimmed. "Hm. Yes. Well, any life-form can seem harmless and adorable, given the right set of circumstances. But let's explore the opposite end of that spectrum."

Elara held her kitten in her hand and hoped against hope that she wasn't called on. Unfortunately, it was almost as if the teacher could sense Elara's discomfort, and soon the robot moved in her direction.

"I see you have selected a young, long-haired cat of mixed breeding," the robot said to the Elara, staring directly into her eyes. "This animal should work well for the demonstration."

And with that, the teacher turned, carrying the tiny crying kitten away.

Elara felt herself gasp. She couldn't help it. But the teacher ignored her and moved toward a laboratory bench at the far end of the room. As she approached, the laboratory lit up, and a large floor-to-ceiling monitor flared to life on the back wall. The monitor displayed an extreme close-up of the tiny kitten in the robot's claw, while another claw extension opened the hatch to a large plexi-steel container and inserted the cuddly creature.

The students may have been mind-controlled, but Elara felt like she could sense some tension. That's when she realized what was happening. This entire exercise was a stress test. The faculty was trying to see if anyone would break free of their mental condition. Which made it all the more important for Elara not to break.

"The kitten . . . ," Elara heard herself whisper.

"It's okay," Sabik reassured.

"We have to trust them," Knot added.

"They keep us safe," Beezle said, compassionate and kind, her words revealing just how powerful a hold the mind control had over her. Over all of them.

On the screen, the students could see that the miniature biosphere was filled with blue and yellow plants and a rocky orange landscape.

"Students," the teacher continued. "As you can see, the animal is having difficulty adapting to its new environment."

It was true. Elara felt herself grow sick. The atmosphere of the biosphere was clearly not comfortable for the tiny creature. But . . . what could she do? How could she stop this? Elara noticed that the students seemed uncomfortable. There wasn't an outcry, but it was clear that some empathy for the poor little creature was burning its way through the classroom.

The teacher adjusted a few controls. The lights flickered as the image on-screen zoomed in closer on the kitten. Elara restrained herself. Her head continued to hurt, and she felt that strange burning sensation behind her eyes again. She looked down at her hands . . .

. . . they were glowing.

"Not now," Elara said in a hushed tone. She sat on her hands. "Whatever this is . . . Not. Now."

Meanwhile, the experiment continued. The kitten in the biosphere tank looked tired. Weak.

"Excellent," the teacher said, her digital expression

reading as smug. "Now, as you will see, there is no cause for concern. Yes, the environment is far too radioactive for the animal. But with the right approach, you will see that such limitations . . . can be conquered."

Another press of a button and green gas filled the biosphere. The kitten began scampering around trying to run away. But there was nowhere to go. Elara tried to look away, but all of her classmates . . . even her friends . . . were just watching.

Elara felt her hands grow warmer. Reaching into her pocket, she grabbed the chrono-hopper. It was still inactive, but holding it tightly seemed to calm her.

The teacher continued to lecture. "Rapid genetic modification is, of course, a last resort when adapting life-forms for a new environment. And has not been used for centuries . . ."

The gas was having an effect on the kitten. It shook fiercely, its tiny head angled upward in a tiny roar. The kitten's paws began to grow, doubling in size in a fraction of a second. Multiple spines erupted from the kitten's back, and its tail grew twice as long and became whiplike. Its eyes grew larger and took on a sinister slant, just as its little baby teeth were replaced with heavy-looking tusks.

". . . But we have to ask ourselves 'why?'" the

teacher continued. "We have a tool here that will help save lives. We can spend years altering a planet's geosphere, and that is always ideal. But sometimes, when necessary, we can instead focus on adapting the life-form to the planet."

The last bits of green gas dissipated. Where there had once been a kitten was now a ferocious-looking monster—admittedly, still only a couple of inches long, at the very most.

"Now open your books, class. Today we will study the effects of controlled radiation and genome sequencing on animal life-forms."

Even as her temples throbbed with a headache, Elara felt a chill.

CHAPTER 010

At the end of class everyone lined up and returned their kittens to the large container, which the robot teacher promptly closed.

"Next time," the teacher said, "you will all have an opportunity to experiment on the animals and see what form of rapid adaptations you can prompt." A smile appeared on the robot's digital face as she continued smugly, "You will see. It will be a true learning experience."

The class filed out in perfect order. Despite the sheer horribleness of what they had just witnessed, the group of students seemed perfectly comfortable. Elara thought she could play along. But after this, it became clear that she couldn't just sit by and not try to change things.

"You guys . . . ," Elara said to her friends as they were walking to the next class, "you guys don't think that was a little . . . I dunno . . . cruel? I mean, that tiny kitten."

"Oh," Beezle said, surprised. "Oh . . . I suppose it was. But it was for the best, I'm sure. Otherwise our teachers would not have engaged in such activities."

Knot scratched her head noisily but sounded unsure. "We have to trust, right?"

Elara shook her head vehemently. Maybe she had a chance. Maybe she could get through to them. "We're supposed to be studying bioengineering!" Elara let out through gritted teeth. "Rapid cellular mutation goes against the very principles of the Seven Systems School! Whatever happened to 'do no harm'?! I mean, we're only a half-step away from the terraforming bombs of the Frils!"

Sabik rubbed his eyes. "Those kittens . . . They were just . . ."

Knot shook her head. "No, Elara . . . You said we

weren't going to go through this anymore. We have to trust the system! Respect it! We can't have a repeat of last year!"

"But . . . ," Elara muttered. She stared at her friends, who all seemed genuinely confused by her concern.

"Elara?" Beezle asked. "Are you feeling unwell-ish? Should we take you to the medical bay?"

There was so much Elara wanted to say. But there was no point.

"I have a headache. Go ahead, I'll catch up later."

Back in her dorm room, Elara winced. She had a headache. A furiously pounding headache. She took the chrono-hopper out of her pocket. The device was still dormant.

She dropped it on her bed and sat down, rubbing her face furiously, trying to make the burning sensation fade. She looked down at her hands. They were glowing again—just a little bit. Elara had already uprooted the plants that had suddenly grown everywhere in her room overnight. But now there were new vines popping up along the walls, glowing faintly for just a moment as they grew.

"What is happening to me?" Elara whispered to herself.

After a moment, the headache faded. Her hands

stopped glowing. She looked at the chrono-hopper. Maybe . . .

All of this had started after Groob had showed up. After Elara got a hold of the chrono-hopper.

There had to be a connection. The chrono-hopper had to be the key.

The door to the common room she shared with Suue slid open with a hiss. Elara poked her head out of her bedroom to see the perpetually mean expression that Suue always seemed to wear. The chrono-hopper was still in Elara's hands. If the device was protecting Elara, maybe she could use it to help others break free of the mind control.

And hey, if it didn't work, better to find out by trying it on Suue.

"Hey . . . Suue?" Elara asked awkwardly, a forced smile at her lips.

Suue stared at Elara like she had an extra set of heads. "Why are you even talking to me?"

Well . . ., Elara thought, *good to know that mind control doesn't stop people from being snobby.*

"Um . . . just a quick question for you," Elara answered. "Today in class. Those tiny kittens. You liked them, right?"

"They were adequate," Suue said, the exasperation in her voice thick.

"Well . . . didn't what happened . . . ," Elara prompted, "didn't it make you feel bad?"

"It . . ." Suue looked like she felt uncomfortable. "It was science. That's what I'm here to learn. Because I'm going to be important and famous—unlike you!"

Elara nodded in agreement as she adjusted a dial on the chrono-hopper. "So . . . what do you think about"—she raised the device quickly, pressing the button and firing directly at Suue—"after I do this?!"

Unfortunately, the chrono-hopper didn't fire anything. Instead, it made a wheezy noise and sputtered, sending a small puff of black smoke into the air.

"Dang," was all Elara could manage to say.

Suue just glared at Elara, her mouth hanging open in disgust.

"You are such a freak," the mean girl said, and then she walked into her bedroom and closed the door.

The next day started with jogging. Then the pledge. Then a class on solar energy conversion and one on geological reconstruction.

Then there was a bell, and the headmistress appeared in every classroom.

"Great news, students!" the hologram announced cheerfully. "We have been monitoring your progress very carefully and are now certain that you are ready for your first field trip! One of the many benefits of our mobile schoolship is being able to take you directly to the very kind of worlds you might one day help transform into a habitable ecosystem! So, please, everyone come to lecture Room 21b for your assignment!"

Elara looked around as students shuffled out. Nearby, Knot grinned. "This is great! A field trip already!"

"Are we. . . . ready for that?" Elara asked hesitantly.

Sabik shook his head. "We must be! Or we wouldn't be assigned to go! Remember, trust!"

"Trust," Beezle agreed.

"Trust," the entire classroom intoned at once.

Soon everyone was assembled in the lecture room 21b, as instructed. A teacher-bot Elara hadn't seen before floated in the center of the room above an elevated platform. It was painted with the military-style uniform and had three heavy limbs attached to its frame.

"Cadets," the robot began. "I am EMJ-71, your instructor in survival training. Your education up until this year has been limited. It has left you weak. Vulnerable. Easy to exploit."

The robot slowly rotated as it spoke so that all the students could have a view of the teacher's face.

"Some of you may have been on missions to other worlds. Little field trips where you ran around and played with soil samples and collected rocks or twigs for study."

One of the robot teacher's metal tentacles pressed a button. A part of the wall opened up and a large view screen was revealed. On it, the surface of an alien word was displayed—a brightly colored, orange-and-green swirling planet.

"Understand that terraforming is NOT an art! It is a means to an end. A matter of survival! The development of new worlds is key to preventing extinction!" The robot pressed another button, and several lights appeared on the image of the planet.

The teacher floated off the platform as a holographic planet hovered above the students. "We are now in orbit around a world ripe for terraforming. But it is filled with dangerous life-forms! Each one of these lights represents a potential threat to your existence. But understand, these threats will make you stronger! When you come out of this, you will be a better, more efficient member of our Galactic Affiliation." The teacher raised its tentacles in a way that mimicked flexing its arm muscles. "You will be safer because of what you will endure! Do I have your trust in this?"

"We trust!" yelled the collective students. "We respect! We obey!"

"And you will be safe!" yelled the teacher back at the excited students.

"Excellent," he said, pressing a button. The image on screen zoomed in on a specific section of the planet, one filled with rocky canyons and boiling volcanoes. "All of you will be transported to the surface of this world. You will be outfitted with survival suits and stun lasers. Your mission is to subdue the creatures that were displayed on the world map. The first student to do so will be rewarded appropriately. The rest will face punishment. Understood?"

One student raised her hand. "How will we be punished?" It was Sapple asking, her many eyes blinking lightly as she spoke.

In response, the teacher glared at the student. The lights flickered as he answered. "How, you ask? Unpleasantly." The teacher turned and cast his gaze over the entire body of students. "I will leave the rest to your vivid, young imaginations. I assume that should be a significant motivation?"

The class grinned, unconcerned with the potential threat. "Yes sir!" they answered in unison.

The teacher smiled. "Excellent. Please divide

yourself into groups. Each group will be given a different departure port. So”—the robot clapped its tentacles together—“suit up and arm yourself. Your training mission begins . . . now.”

The students filed out of the room and into the hangar where their survival suits and weapons waited. Elara fell into step behind Knot, Beezle, and Sabik. Knot was carrying Clare on her back in a harness. “Hey, um . . . ,” Elara said hesitantly. “How are you guys feeling? I mean . . . this mission . . . ?”

All four of Elara’s closest friends turned toward her in tandem. All four opened their mouths to speak at exactly the same time. They looked at one another and laughed. “We’re fine,” Knot said.

“Never better,” added Sabik.

“How are you?” Beezle asked, her brow knitted with concern. “Is something . . . wrong?”

“No . . . Nothing,” Elara said, choking back her horror. “We’re all fine. Everyone is . . . fine,” she lied.

The students lined up and gathered at the docking bay as instructed. Everyone was wearing full space suits to filter out dangerous elements and regulate temperature and oxygen. They were all equipped with a stun laser pistol—the same kind they had trained with every day in munitions class, as well as a series of gas grenades. They were as ready as they

could possibly be—except there was no way to get to the planet.

"Maybe the shuttle hasn't docked yet?" answered an equally confused Beezle.

"Didn't you guys read the ship specs?" Sabik responded, tapping at a wall console. "The schoolships aren't equipped with shuttlecrafts."

"Then how do we get to the surface of the planet?" Elara said, looking around. The hangar was clearly designed so ships could fly and land at need. Only . . . there were no ships.

"Is it . . ." Knot looked around, her voice growing hushed. "Molecular transports? Does this ship have that?"

Beezle shook her head. "I do not believe any such form of transportation exists."

"You mean like . . . teleport?" Elara asked, beginning to wonder herself.

"No . . ." Sabik rolled his eyes. "That stuff is all, like, science fiction. Look—"

He tapped another button, and a large metal tube rose from the floor, causing Elara to stumble back.

"What is that?!" she asked. "That looks . . . awesome."

"Oh!" Beezle said, tilting her head. "That is a high-speed gravity transport tube. Not unlike an elevator, really."

“An elevator through space, plummeting toward a planet at a super-high speed, with no cables or brakes?” Elara asked, raising an eyebrow.

Beezle nodded her head. “It has a gravity-based braking system, but otherwise you are correct.”

“It’s less awesome now,” Elara muttered.

“It’s perfectly safe,” Sabik said, shrugging. “It must be, or the headmistress wouldn’t let us ride in them.”

“This is truth,” Beezle said, smiling. She pressed a button, and several more tubes appeared—one for each of them. “Shall we?”

Elara really did not want to go. But there were few other choices. Besides . . . this was a rare opportunity to get her friends away from the ship.

“Let’s do this!” she said.

The ride was not smooth. Also not long. It was not long because it was horribly, horribly fast. Elara was pretty certain she screamed every second of the way. Her eyes opened briefly when her skin began to feel hot. She glanced down at her hands. Glowing. Of course.

“No!” she said to herself. “Not this! NO!”

And then the small tube slammed into the ground with a thud. Elara expected to be smooshed, but instead, very little shock traveled into the cabin. The transport device worked as promised.

"Phew . . . ," Elara said to herself, frantically pushing the button to open the door. The hatch opened with a hiss, and she staggered out of the pod, taking a step onto the strange, alien world.

And, of course, she was completely alone. Literally this time.

"Hello?" she called out, her voice muffled by her helmet. The interior of the helmet flashed a display screen showing oxygen levels, as well as the temperatures and other relevant information. But it showed no signs of any other students on the built-in scanner. Elara double-checked her handheld signal booster. Nothing there, either.

"HELLO!" she called out again, her eyes searching across the rocky landscape. There was very little in the way of foliage, and the ground was covered by some kind of mineral dust that appeared to be a mixture of blue azurite and maybe a green malachite. There was no liquid water to be seen, but there was a heavy orange fog in the air that obscured anything more than fifty feet away.

Elara started to feel a little bit of panic. Had the transport tube malfunctioned? Was she alone on an empty world? Was this the end of her adventures?

"HEL—" she started yelling for a third and even louder time.

"Oh," came an unwelcome yet familiar voice through Elara's helmet. The headmistress was speaking. "I'm sorry, Elara Adele Vaughn, but interchannel communications are disabled for this challenge. The mission requires you to collect a living sample before anyone else."

"Okay . . . ," Elara muttered to herself. "I just need to find a life-form and get this over with then. Everything else will have to wait, like always. Now let's see . . . " Elara tapped her helmet. She may not have been able to track the positions of her classmates. But she could absolutely track the location of the nearby life-form. It showed up on her helmet screen as a giant yellow dot blinking in and out across the terrain. The signal booster had its own screen that showed more detail. It was close.

"Ha! Got you now. Just over the ridge here," Elara said as she ran up the rocky outcropping. Really, she was starting to wonder if this mission was going to be as challenging as she had been led to believe.

At that moment, the ground underneath Elara's feet exploded. Elara was hurled backward through the air a dozen feet, landing with a heavy thud on her back.

"Wugh," Elara heard herself say. "Blurg," she added,

feeling particularly out of breath from the impact.

Elara opened her eyes, her head still spinning. The planet was really quite beautiful, she thought as she stared upward. You could just see the pink sun peeking through the orange fog. The sky itself was golden due to the atmospheric density, and the giant slavering maw of the monster was looking particularly full of two-foot-long fangs today.

The young girl blinked and looked again. "Yup. Those are the fangs of a giant monster," she murmured to herself. "It's definitely getting ready to eat me, too," she added, trying to get her bruised body to move.

The only part of her that wanted to respond seemed to be her neck. She lifted her head up, and then realized she could wiggle her toes, too. That meant she wasn't really seriously injured, just stunned. It also meant she could feel pain and would definitely be hurting when the giant monster decided to finally take its horrific bite of the terraforming student.

The creature was enormous. Its mouth at least ten feet wide. Its fluffy face was topped with two pointed ears, and large golden eyes flecked with green and black stared down. Its whiskers curled past its face like whips. Its gigantic paws had sword-length claws. It was . . .

". . . Mister Floofyface?"

"Congratulations!" the voice of the headmistress chimed in. "You are the first student to find the target! But you haven't won yet. Please subdue the creature."

Elara finally felt her strength return, just as Mister Floofyface decided that now was the perfect time to strike. The former tiny kitten pounced, its claws raking the spot on the ground where Elara had only just been lying. The twelve-year-old girl fought back her rising panic and reached for her stun gun. As she did, the voice of the headmistress cut back in through the helmet with more useless advice.

"Now, remember what you were instructed to do at the start of the mission! Subdue the creature! Being killed will automatically disqualify you from the session!"

"Point taken!" Elara roared as she fired off her stun gun. "I thought you were supposed to be keeping us 'safe'!"

"Your safety is paramount!" the AI said sweetly. "To ensure that all students are safe, we have designed a program that will eliminate any classmates unable to defend themselves in hazardous situations. This ensures a higher group survival rate!"

The laser bounced harmlessly off the monster. The laser was useless. Elara threw the gun away.

Mister Floofyface swung a heavy paw. The hit sent

her tumbling toward a cliff. Elara skidded and bounced across the surface of the planet, digging her fingers into the grainy blue and green dirt to stop herself from going over the cliff.

She managed—just barely—to hold on to a small rocky outcropping, leaving her thin and somewhat gangly form hanging off the cliff's edge.

Elara's feet kicked, trying to find something to dig into, but it was no use. Her mind raced. She had always heard that you shouldn't look down in this kind of situation because you might panic. Still, Elara was certain that knowing was better than not knowing. She looked down and decided that she was totally ready to panic.

Mister Floofyface looked over the side of the cliff, his giant tongue rolling out in an expression that suggested hunger. Slowly his fangs lowered themselves, ready to pluck Elara from the cliff and swallow her whole.

Elara took a deep breath and said in a very stern, no-nonsense voice, "No! Bad Cat! Bad Mister Floofyface!"

Mister Floofyface reared back, cocking his head in a puzzled expression. Then, seemingly curious, the monster reached down with a paw and prodded Elara. Seizing the opportunity, the girl grabbed the monster's fur and scrambled up the arm and off the edge of the cliff.

Mister Floofyface didn't like that and abruptly tried

to lunge at Elara. But Elara was already on the move, rushing up the monster cat's leg and up to the nape of his neck.

Elara grabbed the thick layer of skin at the base of the creature's neck and pulled as hard as she could. "I know you're a monster now, Mister Floofyface!" she said, straining hard. "BUT YOU'RE STILL . . . A . . . KITTEN!"

The monster howled and hissed. Elara held on, pulling at the spot on every tiny kitten where the mother picks it up to carry.

"SOMEWHERE . . . ," she yelled. "SOMEWHERE INSIDE ALL YOUR MONSTROUSNESS . . . YOU KNOW THIS . . . MEANS . . . I'M IN CHARGE!"

And just like that, it was over. Mister Floofyface dropped to the ground, letting out a surprisingly gentle mewling noise. Then, with a quick motion, the giant monster kitten rolled over onto his back, his paws curled in a docile position, his throat emitting a deep purr.

Elara very carefully stepped forward and stroked the monster's exposed belly. "Shh . . . ," she whispered. "Sleep, little baby kitten. Sleep, Mister Floofyface . . ."

And sooner than Elara would have believed, the monster actually fell asleep.

CHAPTER 011

A laser beam shot out from the distance, narrowly missing both Elara and the sleeping Mister Floofyface.

"Hey!" Elara yelled. "Whoever shot at me . . . it's over! He's asleep, see? I won!"

"I'm sorry, Elara Adele Vaughn," interrupted the voice of the headmistress, "but technically, the monster was not stunned. That means the battle isn't over."

"But that's not fair!" Elara yelled, taking cover from another volley of laser blasts. "The poor thing is asleep! Just end this already!"

"I do not understand," the headmistress answered. "You sound like you do not trust our judgment."

"Oh . . . really?" Elara shouted back, her sarcasm unmistakable. "What gave you that idea!"

Another laser struck the outcropping. A quick spark flared, and her ear filled with a short shriek of static.

Elara grabbed her laser from the ground and took a quick peek over the rock, peering out into the orange fog. Several shady forms were approaching. Elara felt her heart grow heavy even as her head started pounding with the worst headache yet. She knew who the headmistress had sent to come after her. Their silhouettes were unmistakable. The hulking form of Knot. The short and four-armed Sabik. The hairless and slim Beezle.

"Elara Adele Vaughn," the headmistress said, using Beezle's voice. "We only intended this to be a simple competition. But your inability to trust has forced us to explore harsher methods. Please . . . ," the voice said. "Let us help you."

Elara glanced at Beezle. Her friend's eyes were blank. Her body was there, but Beezle was under control of the headmistress, fully and completely.

"Let my friends GO!" Elara shouted through gritted teeth.

Beezle, Sabik, and Knot all whirled at once in the direction of Elara, raising their blasters. A volley of shots was fired, tearing chunks of rock up where they hit. These weren't stun beams. Not anymore.

In unison, all three intoned, "Safe, Elara. We only want you to be safe."

Elara slammed her laser back in her holster. This was too much. This was not happening. The brainwashing was one thing. But this was insane. "Guys!" she called out. "Guys . . . come on . . . it's me! Elara!"

The answer was a barrage of laser fire, narrowly missing the desperate girl. Having ducked back behind the rock, Elara weighed her options. Stand up and get shot, or shoot her friends.

Those were both terrible choices, so she opted for a third path—run away.

Moving fast, Elara scrambled up a crest, trying to move as far away from her friends as possible. As she reached the top, one of the laser blasts sizzled past her leg, burning it badly.

Elara gritted her teeth as she stumbled, the pain lancing all the way from her toes to her hip.

Leaping back up to her feet, Elara desperately tried to think of a plan—any plan. But nothing was coming to her except running. She had thought she would have more time. That somehow on the planet, the power of the mind control would weaken.

Lasers sizzled past—close enough to give her concern, not close enough to hurt. The terrain was rocky and cramped—almost mazelike. Lots of places to hide, but not for very long. No deep caves. No hidden spaceships for escape.

"Elara Adele Vaughn," called out a voice using Beezle to communicate again. "You do not need to run. We only want to help you."

Elara ducked left and zigzagged right. Another voice called out from a different direction—this time it was Sabik, but not really Sabik. "We want to bring order to chaos. To establish a rule that is safe and prosperous for all."

Though it was enormously difficult, Elara didn't yell back. Her friends . . . the mind controlling them . . . were trying to flush her out. If they really didn't want to hurt her, they wouldn't be firing lasers at her.

Her leg burned, and she couldn't help but limp. "A plan . . . ," she whispered to herself as she sped through the rocky maze. "I need a plan . . . think. Think think think—OH! I got it!"

She heard heavy footsteps storming toward her. But still she had an idea. Her friends were hypnotized.

They were being controlled through some sort of hive mind. But Beezle is already part of a hive mind. With a boost, she should be able to shake off the effects of the conditioning, allowing the OverMind to reassert itself.

And if Beezle could make psychic connection to Clare, who was a giant living data-storage cube, the rest should take care of itself. The entire class could be un-brainwashed!

Why had it taken her so long to think of this? She could have done this days ago. Weeks ago! Now there was a chance. Now there was hope.

And that's when a laser blast came out of nowhere, striking dangerously close.

"Well," Elara said to no one in particular. "That's really, really bad."

A smug-sounding voice interrupted Elara's private monologue. "Elara Adele Vaughn . . . ," the voice of the headmistress said through the mouth of yet another student. "You should not resist us. Ours is the way of peace."

Elara looked up. She already knew who the owner of the voice was: mean girl Suue Damo'n, ruining everything as usual. *Great. . . . more lasers to dodge*, she thought sourly.

Elara rubbed her eyes and got ready for a fight, even

as her headache grew stronger than ever.

Behind her, Elara sensed the arrival of her friends. She knew their blasters were raised—set to the absolute highest setting. In front of her stood her archrival in school—the meanest girl she had ever met—Suue Damo'n.

Elara felt her leg burn. Her shoulder was stiff from her fall. Her head was pounding, like a rhythm. Like a drumbeat . . . Over and over and over.

"Elara Adele Vaughn," came the voice of the headmistress through the mouth of Suue. "We are sorry we could not be of assistance and that you find your new environment uninviting. Goodbye."

Elara wasn't sure if it was the threat of her own death, the thought of her friends left to the mercy of a sinister government, or the snotty smirk on Suue's face. But whatever it was, Elara had had enough.

The mind controlling Suue wasn't ready for the charge. Elara slammed into her at full force. Her mind-controlled friends fired a volley of lasers, but they were too late. Elara and Suue went over the cliff's side, plummeting to their probable doom.

CHAPTER 012

Hurling herself off a cliff should have made Elara afraid. Instead, she was too busy wishing the nightmare of her headache would end.

"Stop it!" Elara yelled, feeling like her brain was on fire. "Stop IT!"

Everything seemed to slow down. The ground was maybe twenty or thirty feet below—Elara could finally see it. She had vaguely hoped to see a massive lake below or maybe a perfectly placed trampoline.

No luck. Just giant stone spikes.

Not that she cared. All she could think about was her blinding headache. "Stop . . . ," she cried to no one in particular. "STOP . . . STOPPP!"

And then she exploded. Energy poured from every cell of her body. Like fire, but it didn't burn. It was . . . amazing. It felt almost as if time had stopped, and Elara was outside herself looking in. Waves of strange energy were emanating from Elara. She suddenly felt better than she ever had in her life.

And then time started moving like normal and she was falling again. She closed her eyes and waited for the inevitable sounds of her own body smooshing into the spiky landscape below.

Instead, she splashed into a deep pool of crystal clear water.

Swimming to the top and gasping for air, Elara looked around in confusion. Everything . . . everything was wrong. Everything was . . . different.

Suue splashed up out of the water. "What the heck was that?!"

"I don't know!" Elara yelled back.

"Where did this water come from?" Suue yelled even louder.

"I still don't know!" the equally shocked Elara yelled in response. "And . . . and there's grass . . . and trees.

Are we in a garden?"

Elara was so excited, she almost forgot she was floating in water. *"Pff!"* Elara said, spitting out a mouthful of the freshest water she had ever tasted. "Hey!" She squinted at Suue. "Are you . . . you? Are you normal again?!"

"Ugh!" Suue said back, with a condescending tone. "You are asking ME if I'M normal? For real?"

Elara grabbed Suue in a massive hug. "You're back!" she screamed happily. "You're back and you're awful just like always!"

Suue splashed Elara, snarling just a little. Then she stopped. "Omigosh," she said quietly. "What happened to me? Why . . . why wasn't I . . . me?"

"I know," Elara responded, actually feeling sorry for the horrible girl that she had just thrown off a cliff. "You were mind-controlled. Everyone is. It's . . . something the teachers are doing! Remember the room they took us in?" She glanced around. "Come on . . . let's swim to the shore."

Soon the pair of girls had reached the grassy shore of the oasis. Elara looked at her hands and saw the smallest trace of energy drifting off them, like green sparkly smoke. And then it was gone.

"How did you do all this?" Suue asked, her mouth dropped open, reflecting her shock.

“Seriously . . . no idea,” Elara said, wringing water out of her hair that hadn’t existed three minutes earlier. “Listen. Something bad is happening. Not just on our schoolship, but I think . . . like . . . everywhere. I have an idea to break everyone free from the mind control, but we need to get back to the ship. If we get back to the ship, we can figure something out!”

“But the others . . . they’ll know I’m not mind-controlled anymore,” Suue answered, uncertainty in her voice. It was an odd thing for Elara to hear. She had often believed the mean girl only had two settings—condescending and awful.

“They won’t if you play along!” Elara hissed. “And you have to play along, or else they—”

The voice of the headmistress through the comm system interrupted the conversation. “Elara Adele Vaughn? Our sensors indicate you still live. Please let us know if this is true so we may assist you further.”

“They’re going to find us!” Suue said, panicking.

“Shoot me!” Elara hissed, pulling Suue’s gun hand up toward her chest.

“What?! But—”

“Set it on stun! Tell them you caught me and get us both teleported back to the schoolship. Then they’ll put me in a cell or something and you can break me free!”

“You’re insane—”

“I have a plan!” Elara interrupted, knowing they were almost out of time. “Shoot me now before it’s too late!”

“I mean . . . what if I—”

Exasperated, Elara yelled at Suue, “Your face is stupid, and you smell like cheese!”

And with that, Suue pulled the trigger.

“There,” Elara said. “Was that so—”

And then she fell over, totally unconscious.

Elara woke up, several hours later, strapped to a medical table. The room was brightly lit, with a scanner of some kind on a retractable arm. Elara could see a massive wall-size monitor across the room, despite being restrained.

“Wurgh,” she said.

A robot floated over—one Elara hadn’t seen before. It was painted with a large medical symbol on either side and had several metal arms coming out of its back. These were outfitted with an array of rather frightening-looking medical tools that Elara decided not to focus on. One arm particularly caught Elara’s attention—mainly because it looked fairly silly. It was a folding mechanical arm with a gloved hand at the end. Each fingertip had a different glowing light attached.

A sudden flash of blue light announced the

holographic arrival of the ship's computer. "Ah!" came the uncomfortably familiar voice of the headmistress. "You are awake! How wonderful! We have so many questions for you! V3-ED01, please begin the interrogation."

"Your mind is strong," the robot said. "But no carbon-based life-form can resist the hypnotherapy the way you have. How do you do this?"

The robot moved closer. Elara glanced and saw the many medical attachments. Buzzing saws and long needles and all kinds of nastiness. She held her breath, steeling herself for what was to come. Luckily, the robot chose the silly light-up glove attachment. Elara breathed a massive sigh of relief.

The robot tapped Elara's arm with one glowing fingertip. She felt her arm tingle where it made contact. In the back of her mind she heard a familiar faint rhythmic pounding—like something buried deep that she couldn't quite reach.

"Your cellular structure is unique," continued V3-ED01. "There is an unfamiliar energy signature within your DNA. Why is this?"

Elara felt another fingertip. This time it felt like a freezing spike was driving through her mind. "AAH!" she felt herself cry out, despite her determination not to speak.

The robot reached down below the table and picked up an object. Elara's heart sank when she saw it was the chrono-hopper.

"This device is familiar," the robot continued. "This device is not of this time. How did you come into the possession of this?"

Elara tried to fight back the words, but they were starting to slip out. "It . . . it was . . . given to me."

"By who?" she was asked, feeling the touch of another fingertip. "You will answer," the robotic voice continued.

Elara could barely think. Her headache was back. She was about to break, she could feel it. She still didn't understand why she was immune to the mind control, but whatever gave her immunity, she was just about at her limit.

The screens across the room flickered to life, every inch of them filled with a sinister masked face. "As you can see," the robot said, turning to address the Watchman, "the subject has proven usually resilient to the Hypnoticon Broadcaster, and none of the standard psychotropic compounds have any meaningful effect. It's as if her cellular structure was metabolizing the compounds as soon as they entered her bloodstream."

The robot held the chrono-hopper up for the Watchman to see. "Normally, we would have followed protocol and discontinued her. However, the device she is carrying . . . it does not match the technology of this era."

The Watchman stared silently for what felt like an eternity. "Interrogate her," he said, with a voice that was firm and commanding. "Take her mind if you must, peel away every layer, but find out what she knows."

Elara could tell from his icy tone that the Watchman meant business. She needed to say something . . . anything . . . that would buy her some time. And since the Watchman was clearly a time traveler, maybe dropping the name of another might cause a distraction . . .

"Groob," Elara hissed, feeling the name escape her lips. For a moment, nothing happened. The Watchman just stared at her, and the robot and headmistress AI waited for orders. Then, after a long silence, the Watchman whispered a very angry question.

"How?" he asked, his voice mixed with surprise and rage. "How do you know that name?!"

"Oh . . . I know a lot of things!" Elara yelled back, having absolutely no idea why mentioning Groob had worked. "And I know you're a time traveler, and I know you don't belong here! And if you know what's good for you, you'll go back to whatever future you came from . . . right now!"

The Watchman ignored Elara, shifting his focus to the droids. "Prepare your ship for my arrival. I will conduct this interrogation personally, and then . . . then we will get answers from this . . . child."

Elara felt the sting of another lit-up fingertip. But it no longer bothered her. The Watchman was coming here. That meant she would have a chance. Somehow . . . someway . . . she had to stop the evil time traveler from taking over everything.

Her skin was burning, and the flashing colored lights were making her dizzy. But she held on, wincing as they raced through her system. The rhythmic drumming was starting to build in her head. A surge of energy was building inside her. The weird power that had erupted from her fingertips when she dove off the cliff, instantly terraforming the land around her . . . she knew what it was now. The terraforming marble she had deactivated last year. The one she had swallowed. It had done something to her. It had given her . . . power! The power to instantly rearrange the atomic properties of physical matter. It was hers! And with all that power at her fingertips, no evil robots or galactic conquerors could stop her!

The monitors had powered off, but the robot still hovered over her. "You want answers . . . ?" she whispered, her brow furrowed with intense concentration. "Well . . . here they come!"

She angled her hands up, ready to unleash the powers infused within her.

Nothing happened.

She tried again. This time wiggling her fingers more.

"Dang it . . . ," she muttered to herself as the robot watched her, confused. "Erg . . . ," she added, straining really hard to make the energy stuff explode again.

"Hm," the robot said. "Please take note, the subject appears to be suffering from some sort of delusional state . . ."

"It's really quite embarrassing to watch," the headmistress responded.

At that moment, a wave of energy did spread through the room, but it was a pale green flash of light and it didn't come from Elara at all. Suddenly the robot started sputtering and sparking. So did the computer panels scattered throughout the lab. Even the restraints holding Elara shuddered, snapping open in response to the force.

The holographic headmistress seemed most affected by the unexpected attack. Her face scrunched up impossibly small, then her head expanded to a ridiculously large size. "Blurgle!" she said, unintelligibly. "The pudding is on the moon!" she added, before her projected form was deactivated.

Woozy and rubbing her wrists, Elara looked up. Suue was in the room, having crept in through an open door at the far end of the lab. And she was holding a large, boxy-looking machine with two blinking lights on it.

"Suue!" Elara said, struggling to speak as her head swam. "You did it! You stopped them! We're safe!"

"Yeah . . . about that? I used an electromagnetic pulse generator," Suue responded, her usual frown heavy on her face. "It was the only thing I could find on short notice. Creates an electric short in anything technological. So . . . good for taking out evil robots. Bad for the whole ship."

Elara was impressed, though still somewhat confused. "That's . . . that's great!" she said. "Again . . . we're safe!"

Suue rolled her eyes. "Ugh. You so didn't pay attention to anything last year. We're still in a planet's gravity well. So . . . the ship? With no power? No engines?"

"Oh," Elara responded, suddenly understanding. "That's the bad part. We're totally going to crash. Like, to our deaths."

"Yeah." Suue nodded. "That's pretty much what I'm saying."

CHAPTER 013

Elara and Suue rushed through the ship, passing disabled robots and disoriented students at every turn. The entire massive, saucer-shaped vessel was listing heavily to one side, leaving the floors steeply tilted. This was an effect of the ship slowly being dragged down by the gravity of the planet they had been orbiting.

"Did you have to take out the whole ship?!" Elara shouted while running.

Suue rolled her eyes. "Oh . . . because you were doing SO great on your own, is that it?"

A computer panel near the pair sparked as they ran past. Elara veered through a corridor to the left.

"The engine room is the other way!" Suue shouted, trailing five feet behind Elara while struggling to carry the heavy pulse generator.

"We can't restart the engines on our own!" Elara yelled back. "We need help!"

"But everyone's either a robot or a zombie!" Suue shouted. "There's nothing we can do! If we can't start the engines, then we need to abandon ship!"

Elara skidded to a halt, whirling on Suue. "My friends are on board! Your friends are on board, too! Scrubby and Peter and Silent Dave! Would you seriously just leave them behind?!"

" . . . Enh?" Suue said, looking like she was mentally weighing the pros and cons.

Elara decided she didn't want to hear any more of the mean girl's answer. "Look, this is way more than one ship! This is our entire government! If we abandon ship, we'll just get picked up by the next crew of mind-controlling future robots! So . . ." She suddenly pointed at a door. "This is it! The dorm room area! Help me open it! We need to get Beezle, and we need to access a computer station!"

Suue grabbed at the door and pushed. "But the mind control?" she yelled, straining hard to get the door open. "Everyone is brainwashed, remember?"

"I think it's all some kind of electric web," Elara answered. "The hypno machine should be offline like everything else!"

"Do you know that for fact?"

"Of course I don't!"

The two girls pulled at the heavy door, finally forcing it open.

Elara was the first to enter the room, seeing exactly what she expected to find in the common room: her friends, collapsed on the floor, weak and disoriented. Meanwhile, Suue rushed over to a computer station and started ripping off the external housing.

"Beezle!" Elara yelled, grabbing her Arctuiaan friend who had somehow managed to collapse in a way that left her dangling off a table. "Beezle, wake up! We need your help!"

"Hello, Elara," Beezle muttered, semiconscious, her eyes flittering open. "Why am I upside down?"

"Good!" Elara shouted. "You're you again! Listen . . . you need to hack into the schoolship's computer system and override the controlling program for the headmistress! You need to reprogram her, and you need to do it right now!"

"But . . . ," Beezle was confused and disoriented. Her words slurred as she spoke—a clear side effect of the mind control. "Interfering with the headmistress AI program could compromise the ship. I would not wish to endanger us in any way."

"We're already crashing toward a planet," Elara pointed out.

"I see," Beezle responded, abruptly more awake. "Well. I do very much dislike being reduced to fiery wreckage. I will do this thing you ask."

Beezle staggered upward, struggling to adjust to the uneven floor. She looked confused again. "Wait . . . why does the headmistress require reprogramming? Is she broken in some way?"

Suue was trying desperately to rewire a control panel into the EMP generator. "She's a mind-controlling goob!" the mean girl shouted.

Beezle looked over at Suue and then back at Elara, a puzzled look on her face. Then suddenly her eyes lit up as she stared at her friend. "Oh no! That explains why I was trying to destroy you! I did think that was very strange!" Her eyes then became damp. "I am so sorry! I know we were fighting, but I promise to never try to kill you with lasers again!"

"It's okay!" Elara shouted as she felt the ship shudder. They were closing in on the planet's atmosphere. Time was growing short. "Just reprogram the headmistress so she isn't evil, then we can take control of the ship!"

"We have power at this station!" Suue yelled as a series of sparks shot across the cabin.

Beezle glanced around. "We will need Clare," she said. "I can access the ship's drive system, but Clare's data-processing ability is much greater."

Elara found the yellow rectangular sponge leaning against a nearby table. "Sorry, Clare!" she said, pushing the top of the life-form over so that she fell flat onto the hull with a loud *foomp*. With the tilt of the floor, it was easy enough to drag her across the room.

Beezle quickly clipped a series of loose wires from the console to Clare, then laid down on the yellow sponge's surface as if taking a nap.

"Clare is still unconscious," Beezle explained as she closed her eyes and made herself comfortable. "I will guide the interface myself. I will need to navigate the operating system of the simulated headmistress. This means sorting through thousands of layers of data, all compressed into a binary machine language. It will be quite difficult and time-consuming."

"What?!" Suue said.

"Time-consuming?!" Elara added.

"We're going to die!" both girls wailed.

At that moment, Beezle opened her eyes and

blinked. "I am done," she said. "I am so very sorry . . . it took even longer than I anticipated."

The lights of the cabin flared back on. Hoping for the best, Elara yelled, "Headmistress! We need help!"

A blue flash filled the room, and the headmistress appeared—though far less rendered than before. Instead of appearing as a polished representation of a living being, she looked more like a kindergartener's crayon scribble taped to a refrigerator.

"Squaaakkk!" chirped the very broken headmistress AI. "I got all the pananacakes! Whoooop!"

"That's . . . not super good," Elara admitted.

"I removed over seventy-five percent of her original programming. It was all quite evil and rude," Beezle explained. "But she should still function—at least in a rudimentary fashion."

"Whoawhoawhoawhoa!" the hologram screeched as a computer monitor activated. "That's a BIIIIIIG planet!"

"Yes!" Elara yelled. "Yes, it is! And we're totally going to crash into it unless you do something! Can you do something?"

"Hm," the hologram responded in a grave manner. "Yes. Yes I can. I can so very much do something."

"Okay!" Elara nodded. "Great! So—"

"Oh!" the hologram interrupted with a tone of

dawning realization. "You mean can I do something to save everyone on this ship from crashing into the planet! Hm . . . no. No, sorry. That sounds hard to do with holographic hands. You'd need to activate the manual override on the bridge. But I can't do that because I can't touch anything."

"Ah," Elara said in quiet response.

"But what I can do . . . ," the bizarre headmistress said, "is DANCE."

Suue slammed her head on the console. "Why didn't I just evacuate?!" she muttered, accenting each word with a hard knock of her head.

"BowchickawwaaWAA!" the headmistress sang while running in place and shaking her fists.

Elara looked around. According to the data on the monitor, the ship was in the last stages of a decayed orbit. Rotating around the planet faster and faster while edging closer and closer to the surface. They still had a couple of minutes before they reached terminal velocity and ended in a death spiral into the alien world.

"Sabik!" Elara yelled, grabbing the half-conscious Suparian. "You're with me on the bridge! Suue, help Beezle with stuff!"

Elara dragged Sabik out of the door and down the hall. "Wha?" Sabik asked, slowly becoming aware of

his surroundings. "Hey . . . aren't I mad at you? Why should I—"

"Because otherwise we all die!" Elara yelled, pulling Sabik down the hall by one arm.

"Fair enough," Sabik answered.

The two students ran through the halls faster than Elara would have guessed, thanks in part to the tilting ship.

Seconds later, the pair crashed through the doors to the bridge. It was a large circular room with a floor-to-ceiling, 360-degree monitor encircling it. There were several workstations and a captain's chair in the center of the room. It had clearly been built for living beings before it was transformed into a robot ship.

There were a few robots on the bridge, all of which seemed to be malfunctioning. Elara looked around for some sign of an override control. "Okay, the hologram said we need the override—"

"Got it!" Sabik yelled, pulling a broken robot out of the way to reveal a control station with a set of flight controls.

"How did you know to look for that?"

"Well, we're kind of obviously crashing, right?"

"Good point."

The Suparian flicked several toggles and pressed a bunch of buttons, frustrated with the lack of response. “So . . . I just gotta say,” he said as he pulled an unresponsive lever, “if you were trying to prove your point about the dangers of the time-traveling tyrant . . . this is overkill.”

“I tried to warn you all!” Elara snapped as she tried to get the scanner online.

Sabik shook his head. “I knew you were waiting to say that!”

A half second later, several lights activated. “We’ve got some console power!” Sabik yelled, pressing a button. In response, the front wall monitor activated, displaying a full view of the ship deep in the planetary atmosphere, plummeting fast to the surface of the blue-and-green world.

“Hold on!” Sabik yelled, yanking the controls up as tight as they would go. The ship dramatically shifted upward, and Elara tumbled backward through the command center. She slammed to a stop as she hit one of the control stations and, looking up, noticed the surface of the planet still growing larger.

“Why are we still crashing?!”

“We’re . . . in the gravity well!” Sabik yelled through gritted teeth as he kept his pressure on the controls. “It’s gonna get worse before it gets better!”

Elara pulled herself up and staggered to the captain’s chair, where she slapped a ship-wide communicator switch on. "Hey, everyone! This is Elara! Brace yourselves!"

Strapping herself in, Elara glanced at the readout panel of the captain's chair. With a quick tap of the screen, she realized that the ship had an incoming message.

"We have an incoming message!" she yelled.

"Do I look like I care right now?!" Sabik shouted back as he struggled to not hit the planet.

The ship hit another atmospheric bump as Sabik tried again to gain altitude. The ship rocketed upward and then slammed back downward with enough force that Elara almost lost her breath. Not knowing what else to do, she pressed the button to open the comm channel with whoever was messaging them.

"Schoolship 001," a robotic voice called out. "This is your robotic sentry patrol, assigned to your vessel to ensure your safety!"

Elara felt herself grow pale. "It's the security drones!" she yelled to Sabik, who still wasn't listening. "I completely forgot about them! They were out of range of the EMP!"

"We have detected that your ship's security protocols have been disengaged," the robotic voice continued. "You have thirty seconds to reactivate before you are found to be noncompliant. Noncompliance is a threat to the safety of the Galactic Affiliation. Threats will be met with force. Please, understand that failure to reactivate protocols will result in your destruction.

"Have a nice day!" the robotic voice added cheerfully.

The rearview screens activated, and Elara saw that they were being pursued by three small, triangular-shaped robot starfighters. All of which were preparing to open fire.

CHAPTER 014

"Headmistress!" Elara called out. "Do we have shields?! Please tell me we have shields!"

The hologram flared to life with a blue flash. The holographic image looked just as terrible as before, quickly dashing Elara's hopes that Beezle, Clare, and Suue had managed to improve the AI's functionality.

"Why?" the hologram asked, sulky. "Why does it even matter? Why does anything matter?"

Elara shook her head, irritated that she had even

tried. In response, the hologram stuck out her tongue defiantly and vanished.

Elara hit a button on the command chair, opening a direct channel to Beezle and the others. "Hey! Can you activate the shield from there?" Elara yelled into the comm, trying desperately not to close her eyes as she watched Sabik narrowly miss a mountain.

"We have our own problems, thank you very much!" came the voice of Suue.

"What?" Elara snapped back. "This isn't a competition! We have fighters chasing us!"

"Yeah," Suue snapped back. "And we have your friend Knot trying to smash us into a thousand little pieces!"

"WHAT?!"

Beezle interjected, "The very mean Suue speaks truth, I fear. It seems that the hypnotic systems used on this ship are ineffective against non-carbon-based life-forms, which is why they are all wearing the collars. They serve as an independent control system and are still mentally enslaved."

"Well . . . take it off her, then!"

"We are endeavoring to do so," Beezle said in her usual bubbly and optimistic voice. Snarling and crashing sounds emanated from the background. "Unfortunately, she is trying to eat us, so it may take some time."

With that, the communicator went dead.

The first volley of lasers burned past the ship, which Sabik was still desperately trying to keep from smashing into the planet. The hull of the massive schoolship shuddered. The lights all flashed, and a siren started blaring from somewhere. Elara looked at the control panel desperately. The ship had no shields. No weapons. No means of defense. It was just a school, even if it was flying through space.

And that's when Elara realized there was only one option available—assuming it didn't completely destroy them in the process.

"Sabik!" Elara yelled as she unbuckled herself from the command chair. "Get ready!"

"For what?" he yelled back as another volley of lasers sped past the ship.

"For me to do something incredibly stupid!" Elara shouted as she reached a navigational console. It was all there, just as she hoped. Star charts and space lanes and hyperspace codes . . .

Sabik looked up from what he was doing, his skin fading to grey as he realized what Elara intended. "Oh . . . oh, no you can't! We're in a planetary atmosphere!"

The third round of lasers scored a direct hit. Multiple alarms went off. Elara was barely able to stay seated at the navigational console. Sparks were flying everywhere, and smoke was billowing from one side of the command center.

"We don't have a choice!" Elara yelled, slamming in coordinates she hoped would be safe. "Hold on!"

And with the pull of a lever, Elara activated the massive ship's hyperdrive system, rocketing the vessel through the raw, wild energy of hyperspace to an unknown destination.

Elara held on to her chair. She felt like the velocity was going to pull apart her body, atom by atom. The skin of her cheeks was fluttering as if blown by a massive wind. It was all an illusion—sort of. Punching through unchartered hyperspace lanes meant exposure to raw cosmic energy—the very building blocks of reality. Or so the talking horse that had materialized on the bridge reminded Elara.

"You've got to hit the braaakesss," the horse neighed, just before putting on a fancy tuxedo and tap-dancing off the bridge.

Elara knew that the horse was a hallucination. Just like she knew that she hadn't really just been transformed into a very sad harpsichord with three broken strings.

"NO!" Elara heard herself yell. "I am NOT a harpsichord!" And with every ounce of willpower she had, she forced her hand up to the control panel, reached for the brake lever, and disengaged the hyperdrive engine.

The ship shuddered to a halt, probably shedding a couple of pieces in the process. Elara stood up, then flopped back down, exhausted.

"That . . . ," Sabik said from the pilot's station, "was so cool."

"We've flown through hyperspace before," Elara somehow muttered weakly.

"But we never phased through a planet. That was . . . actually really dumb. We should have completely blown up, probably in the most painful way possible. But we lived, so instead it was really brilliant."

"I did say it was a bad idea," Elara pointed out.

"And you were very right," Sabik said with all the gravity he could muster.

Elara pushed the comm button. "Suue? Beezle?" she asked. "What's our status?"

There was a static hissing noise, then Suue's voice rang through the comm system. "Status? You want the status, like we 'work' for you? Guh! Like, I give you an inch and you get all bossy? Whatever!"

Then Suue hung up.

"Well . . . ," Elara said to Sabik with a shrug, "at least things are getting back to normal."

Elara soon discovered that there was both good news and bad news. The good news was that the schoolship had evaded its pursuers. In fact, sensor data seemed to suggest that the robot ships chasing them were destroyed in the wake of the hyperspace jump. And since the jump was random, it would be super difficult for any other ships to track them. Even more importantly, the core power source was offline. And as long as it was, no one could track them.

The bad news was that the ship was in terrible shape. At best, it was running on low-level emergency power. Not even the lights were at full capacity. The bio-dome had cracked, several pieces of the hull were severely weakened, one of the three engines were ruptured, and about two-thirds of the students had been unable to shake off the mind-control programming. Beezle was certain that over time they would return to normal, but for now they were willing to be locked in the conservatory of the ship while the mind control faded.

Knot, free from hypnotic influence after Beezle and Suue had removed her collar, was feeling particularly guilty. "I'm horribly disappointed in myself," she confided to Elara when the dust had settled. "I know I was under mind control and that none of it was really me, but you must think so little of me now!"

Elara reached out a reassuring hand to caress the Grix's monstrously large, stony shoulder. "It's okay!" she said, trying to make sure her friend felt better. "It literally wasn't you! It was the awful robots and the headmistress and the Watchman . . . they did this. They used you as a puppet!"

"But everything on the planet . . . ," Knot moaned.

"I know!" Elara responded. "It's okay!"

But Knot was inconsolable. "Even mind-controlled, I should be a better hunter than that! I was raised in the blood fields of the Grixicon! I was trained as a baby to leap confidently across the hills and find my prey!" The overwrought stone giant let out a very sweet-sounding sob.

Elara felt her smile freeze on her face. "So . . . um . . . what you're sad about is that you . . . failed to catch me on the planet?"

Knot looked up at Elara, her wide eyes heavy with unshed tears. "Exactly!" the Grix said. "Elara, I love you like a sister and would never ever want to see you hurt . . . but let's be fair. If I had been a proper Grix hunter, you would have been reduced to a pile of stinking flarg within a minute!"

"And . . . uh . . . 'flarg' is . . ."

"Bad!" Knot said with a moan. "You really don't want to be a pile of stinking flarg! Really!"

"Well . . . ," Elara said hesitantly. "Maybe next time you're mind-controlled you will be more . . . efficient?"

Knot smiled warmly at Elara, gently placing her large hand over her friend's own. "I promise . . . ," she answered, "to do so much better if ever given the chance. I won't disappoint you like that again."

"Great?" Elara answered.

Dealing with the robots was relatively easy. Most of them had been permanently disabled by the EMP blast, but at least one of them—Commander X30r—was functioning enough for Elara and her friends to perform an interrogation.

The students had set the robot up in one of the schoolship's hangars—a room with the least amount of accessible technology in case the evil machine had a trick up its sleeve.

Beezle significantly rewired the commander. "It should answer our questions," Beezle said optimistically. "I think I have circumvented its motivational subroutines, but I cannot be certain. It is an amazingly sophisticated machine."

Elara shrugged. "Fire it up."

There was a hissing noise. The robot, which had been lying on the floor of the hangar, suddenly began to hover. Then it crashed back down, rolling back and forth. The screen face showed a zigzag line, and the voice modulator began grunting words.

"You . . . you . . . you are in violation . . . violation . . . ," the robot said, its voice flat compared to before.

"Hold on . . . ," Beezle said, adjusting a data pad she had wired to the robot. The screen face shifted into a very happy smile. "Try now."

"Commander X30r?" Elara started. "What can you tell us about your mission? Why were you brainwashing us?"

"Hello, students!" the commander said in a disarmingly happy voice. "I'm sorry I tried to enslave you all. But orders are orders!"

"Right," Elara pushed. "But . . . why?"

"Woo!" the robot cheered. "All citizens must be ready! Yay! Ready for the onslaught!"

Beezle tapped a few buttons. "I am sorry. It seems that the only personality matrix compatible with answering questions is this ridiculously joyful one. This robot must be happy, or it will not speak with us."

Elara waved away the concern. "It doesn't matter." She took a step closer to the robot. "What do you mean? What . . . onslaught?"

"The the the the the the FRILLIANTH!" the robot said with a distinctly joyful squeal. "They're a-comin! And we gotta stop 'em!"

Elara shook her head while several of her classmates began to murmur. "The Frils are locked away in the time stream. Forever."

"But forever is soooooo long! And today may be okay, but tomorrow will always come!" the robot sang as sparks shot out from its frame. Its screen turned to a frowny face. "The Frillianth tried tried tried already . . . they could try try try again. They could win. Maybe they did win. A long time from now. Explode the gateway explode the gateway garden gate explode!"

And with what sounded like an evil laugh, the robot caught fire. Smoke began pouring from its frame, and it ceased to function.

CHAPTER 015

With only one engine, and a misfiring hyperdrive, the schoolship was forced to limp along the safe and slow subspace lanes. This was fine because no one really knew where to go—other than to stay out of sight. Most everyone on board was either resting, studying, or just trying to have some fun. Elara was feeling stressed and had opted to spend a little time alone in her dorm room playing with Mister Floofyface. Like all the other kittens, Mister Floofyface had been returned to normal kitten size. But there was no way to change the kitten back from his monstrous form. Elara wasn't bothered by it. And for the most part, Mister Floofyface acted just like any other cat. Only his claws were a lot sharper, and his fangs were a lot longer.

A sharp beeping noise interrupted Elara's thoughts. "Come in!" she called out. The door to her room slid open. It was Beezle, and she had an unusual expression on her face.

Elara gently put the kitten down. "What is it now?" she asked. "You look worried."

Beezle hesitated a moment and then stepped inside. The door slid closed behind her. "I was just hoping that it would be acceptable to you to have a difficult discussion."

Elara raised an eyebrow. "About what?"

"I have concerns," Beezle said. "I have concerns about you."

"I'm fine. A few bruises, but—"

"That is not the manner in which I am concerned," Beezle said, holding up a hand as she interrupted. "I do not know if you understand that there were some problems with you . . . from before."

Elara's brow furrowed. "What?" she asked, confused. "What did I do?"

"That you would ask suggests that I am right to be concerned," Beezle said. "Before . . . when you were angry and not speaking with us. You were very difficult. And you were unkind."

"But you were mind-controlled," Elara countered. "All of you. I mean . . . I get it now. You guys didn't want to listen to any warnings or anything. The teachers . . ."

"But we were not mind-controlled then," Beezle argued. "Not at the start. We all remember our actions and words quite well, and those choices . . . they are unaltered."

"But I was right!" Elara glared. "I tried to warn you, but none of you would listen—and look what happened! How many times did we almost die?!"

"What should we have done differently?" Beezle asked, calm where Elara was growing frustrated.

"Listened to me!" Elara shouted.

"And then you would have had us do . . . what?"

"Something!" Elara answered. "Anything!"

"But those are not answers. What specifically would you have had us do?"

"I don't know! I don't know specifically!"

"That is the problem," Beezle answered. "We always believed you. But we did not know what to do, either. Which we did try to tell you. And you got mad at us for that—your friends."

Beezle walked to the door, pressing the button on the side of the wall to open it.

"Elara . . . please understand," she said as she stepped out of the room. "You can be right about something and still act poorly. I am sorry if this offends you. I just believe that it is important to . . . reflect on these things."

The door closed behind her, leaving Elara alone.

Over the next few days, the tensions among the students grew worse and worse. A few of them were feeling that, though they had been mind-controlled, they had been safe. And even though Suue Damo'n didn't agree with that notion, she made it clear that Elara was the worst possible choice to lead the students in their time of need.

"I'm just saying," Suue argued, "that you clearly seem to attract all kinds of drama! Everyone knew it last year . . . and look how all that turned out. If it hadn't been for all your crazy stuff, maybe we'd all still be happy and safe at STS!"

"All I wanted to do last year was learn about terraforming!" Elara snapped back. "It's not my fault that the headmistress wanted to kill me!"

A flash of blue light interrupted the argument.

"Hello!" said the still very broken headmistress hologram, with holographic cake in her arms. "You called and I have arrived! Let us celebrate!"

"Not you, Headmistress," Elara struggled to explain. "I was talking about the other headmistress. From last year. Just . . . never mind."

The hologram hissed at Elara and hurled the cake at the collected students. Which didn't do anything because it was a hologram. With another flash, the AI and her holographic cake vanished.

"Look . . . ," Elara tried to continue. "I don't care who is in charge here. Sabik says the ship is almost ready to run . . . and we need to do something, right? What are our choices?!"

"Hold on . . . ," Sabik interrupted, looking up from the eight-thousand-page ship's manual. "I'm not a mechanic . . . I just, y'know . . . I like ships . . ."

Elara glared at him. "You said this one was almost ready to run!"

Sabik winced. "In the sense that it's not on fire!"

"But . . . ," Elara prompted, hoping for a win. "Pretty soon it will be . . ."

"Still super broken," Sabik said, rubbing engine grease from his hands. "We can fly from one place to another. That's about it."

"All right . . . ," Elara said, rubbing her hands

together. “So what’s not working? What can we do to fix it so that next time we’re attacked—”

“Oh,” Sabik answered. “Oh, no way. If we get attacked again, we’re just little bits of space dust.”

“We need to be able to fight,” Elara snapped back, louder than she intended.

“Or negotiate! Or go home to our families! Whatever!” Suue countered, undeterred. “I can think of lots and lot of things we could do, and probably none of them will lead to our doom. Can you say the same thing?”

“Yes!” Elara shouted. “We can try to stop whatever it is that’s happening! That’s the only choice there is!”

“How is that the only choice?! We’re all kids, flying through space in a broken school! You’re talking about attacking the government?”

“A mind-controlling tyrant from the future is NOT the government!”

“It is if he’s in charge!”

Several kids murmured, and Elara felt the room slipping away from her. But before she could speak again, Beezle made a polite coughing sound, attempting to interrupt.

“I do not wish to cause further strife, but is it not of consequence that we are now considered enemies of the Affiliated Worlds?”

“What?” both girls asked in unison.

"Oh!" Beezle blushed. "It is my fault for forgetting you lack a networked hive mind. Since the mind-control machines have been disabled, I have once more been able to access the Arctuiaan OverMind. It is quite comforting to return to my people in this manner."

"Beezle . . . ," Elara said, sensing her friend was drifting from the point.

"Right!" Beezle said, refocusing. "Through the OverMind, I was able to access certain news sources. It seems that reports indicate that our class has gone mad with power and seized control of our ship, and we are now considered 'highly dangerous criminals.'"

With that news, some of the students became visibly upset. A young Vereerian girl started crying, and one of the two Milos sat down and put his head between his knees. Suue just looked angrier and glared at Elara.

None of this is right, Elara thought to herself. This wasn't how things were supposed to be. For the first time in two years, she really thought about how her crazy adventures—wanted or not—might affect the lives of people around her. She even realized what it must be like for Suue, who saw Elara as privileged with attention where others were so often overlooked.

Elara stepped into the middle of the room. "No . . . Listen," she said. "Suue is right. In a lot of ways, this really is my fault."

She held her hands up and stared at them. She could feel it . . . tingling right below the surface.

"Things happened last year. I didn't want them to happen, but . . . they got out of control. And now . . ."

Her hands began to glow . . . just a little at first, but more and more with each word. Energy drifted off them like steam or smoke. All of the kids watched, even Suue, who had some foreknowledge of the strange power Elara had within herself.

"I'm who the Watchman wants. He wants to protect the galaxy from the Frils, and I . . . I'm somehow the key to all of that stuff. So . . . all of you can go home. No one will be looking for you. Not after they see what I can do."

Elara held her hand forward, palm facing the deck of the ship. As the energy poured from Elara's outstretched hand, metal and rubber gave way to a small patch of grass and flowers.

The entire room went silent for a minute, then everyone started shouting all at once.

"Hang on . . . ," Sabik finally said, standing on the ship's manual so he would be tall enough. "Everyone! HEY!"

Slowly the volume in the room dropped down.

"That . . . ," Beezle said in a hushed tone, "is quite . . . unusual."

"It's . . . yeah," Elara responded. "Something happened to me last year. I had to swallow one of Nebulina's marbles, and the terraforming energy . . ." Elara sighed. "It really doesn't matter. The point is, the Watchman knows that I know he's a time traveler. So, I'm the one he wants. And . . . I think I can make everything better for all of you if I just give up. You know?"

Sabik raised a confused eyebrow. Several other students scratched their heads. Knot blinked, shaking her chin. "Wait," the Grix said, confused. "Are you saying you're going to turn yourself in? Just give up to this bad guy? The one who wants to control minds?"

Elara shrugged. "I mean . . . yeah. I guess I am. That way I can help all of you."

Suue rolled her eyes. "That is just . . . now you're, like, pouring dumb onto stupid."

"Hey!" Knot said, standing up in defense of her friend. "Look . . . she's right, honestly. But still! Be nice, Suue!"

"Why? She's being dumb!" Suue countered, unfazed by the sight of the irritated Grix. "And you all know it! Like, what . . . ? Little miss martyr here is going to bounce on down to the bad guy's house and wish all of this away?! Come on!"

Beezle looked at Elara with a shrug. "Our mean classmate speaks truth. Your idea is quite bad."

Elara's jaw dropped. "Oh, come on!" she said, unsure of what else to say.

Sabik stepped down from the manual, picking the book up with all four hands. "Look, you realize we all had our minds controlled, right? We're all pretty deep in this."

Suue stepped forward toward Elara, her chin thrust out aggressively. "See? Everyone gets it. Everyone but you! The point I was making is that we have, like, lots of choices we can make. And YOU only seem to want to make ones that focus on you! So, we'll ignore you, and do things the proper way: with a vote! Let's decide who gets to run things around here."

And with that, Suue and most of the students filed out to put together a voting box. Sabik and Knot both looked at Elara, shrugged, and followed the rest of them.

Beezle smiled. "I have never voted before! This will be fun!" she said, and followed after Knot.

For a moment, Elara stood alone in the room, staring down at the patch of green she had willed into existence. Then she smiled and followed everyone else. Voting sounded pretty good, after all.

CHAPTER 016

It was just a day later that Elara found herself sitting back in the commander's chair. The ship was still in terrible shape—though a little better than Sabik had suggested.

Sapple had taken over the pilot's station from Sabik. She had more experience than he did, but the Suparian hated to share. The two Milos were working on the scanner systems with Suue's friend Scrubby, while Suue sat at the hyperdrive station, her face locked in its permanent judgmental glare.

Beezle, Sabik, Knot, Clare . . . they were all in position. Elara tapped a comm device plugged into her ear and called out, "You guys comfortable in there?"

"No!" Sabik grumbled back. "This is the worst plan ever!"

"You were outvoted!" Elara heard Knot grumble back at Sabik.

"We are fine, Elara," Beezle said, her voice as bubbly as ever. "Do not trouble yourself with concerns for our comfort. We are with you and ready!"

Elara nodded. "Thanks, guys. Just hold on . . . it will probably get a bit crazy." With that, she disconnected the comm system and patted her jacket pocket gently, feeling something move in response.

Sabik was right. It was probably a terrible plan. But given the circumstances, it was the best plan they had. And the whole student body had agreed to go through with it.

While Elara and her friends manned the captain's chambers, the majority of students paced the ship, doing small repairs and looking for a comfortable spot to sit. Most of them had dug up snacks from the ship's stores, and many had also managed to scavenge some games and comic books.

It was about as professional an operation as anyone could expect from a group of twelve-year-olds who were only recently freed from the clutches of mind-controlling robots.

The ship's primary power core was still offline, but that was going to change very soon.

"Headmistress!" Elara called out.

The blue light flashed, and the hologram came online.

"The potato has pride," the formerly evil headmistress computer program said quite sagely.

"Yes." Elara nodded. "Of course it does. And that is as it should," she added for good measure. Over the last few days, the students had come to realize that it was best to smile, nod, and keep their questions simple.

"I was wondering—" Elara started.

The headmistress quickly interrupted. "Shh . . . ," she said overly loudly. "I can hear you!"

"If maybe . . ."

"Don't be jealous!" the program snapped, flashing brighter blue. "All I can do is wish we were back on the ranch!"

". . . you might be able to activate the primary core?"

The headmistress stopped talking and whirled on Elara. "A quest!" she yelled. Then she opened her mouth, and a small key appeared on her tongue.

"Thoo muth thak thu keh an jhurney thoo thuh thorcerers thair!" the headmistress said with her mouth full.

Elara reached up and grasped the key with her hand. Sort of. It was still only a hologram.

"Why . . . ," Elara asked as the headmistress blinked out of existence, "must a hologram be covered in holographic drool?"

"Best not to wonder," Sapple said while adjusting the navigational systems.

"So gross!" Elara continued, shaking her head. "What am I supposed to do with this, anyway?"

Almost in response, a holographic cylinder rose in front of the command seat. "It has a keyhole!" Elara exclaimed excitedly.

"Kinda figured that," Suue snarked. "So use the key!"

Elara stepped forward and moved the holographic key toward the holographic lock. Miraculously, the full array of lights suddenly flared on. The control panels all blinked, and a general humming noise could be heard from somewhere deep within the ship.

Everything was back online, up and running.

Elara looked around the command deck. Everyone was waiting anxiously to see what would happen. As expected, they didn't have to wait long.

"There's a blinking light," one of the Milos said. "It's a sensor alert!" the other Milo added.

"Scramble the signal!" Suue's friend Scrubby nervously yelped. "Don't let them lock on to our coordinates!"

“We’re okay . . . ,” Elara said in her most reassuring voice. “Remember the plan . . .”

At that moment, the monitors activated. But instead of showing a view of space, the screen was dominated with the masked face of the Watchman.

“Ah,” the Watchman said, a wicked sneer to his voice. “The girl who thinks she knows me.”

“Yeah,” Elara answered, staring at her enemy. “That’s me. Hi.”

The Watchman glared, his angry eyes the only feature visible through the mask.

“I was thinking . . . ,” Elara said. “That maybe we got off on the wrong foot. I mean, you did have me restrained, and your robots were trying to mind-control me. But maybe we’ve just had a misunderstanding?”

The only answer was a soft chuckle. Then the Watchman began to laugh harder. It was as ominous and threatening a laugh as Elara could imagine.

The sinister masked figure folded his hands together, index fingers pointing upward and resting on his chin. “I admit . . . you intrigue me,” the Watchman said. “You possess technology you cannot possibly possess. And you sit here and make jokes . . .”

He leaned forward, the menace in his pose plain to all. “Perhaps you do not understand how little effort it took for me to seize control of your government, or how quickly I eliminated all who would oppose me."

He tapped a button. "Soon enough, I will have a lock on your coordinates. You think you can bargain or play games? You will be under my power soon, all of you."

The ship shuddered, and the lights flickered.

Elara stood up, walking slowly and menacingly toward the screen. For the plan to work, they would need every second of time they could get, and her courage and confidence had to be unshakeable.

"You know what I think?" Elara asked the masked man, her back to the students on the bridge. "I think you're scared. You come from the future and you bring all this technology with you to take things over, and what?" She pushed, feeling bold. "Some kid who knows what you are waltzes in and takes out your mind-controlling schoolships and three of your robot drone fighters?"

The Watchman snorted with contempt. "You are only a child . . ."

The ship shuddered again. "Yeah . . . we all are," Elara replied, grinning. "I was actually just thinking about that. See . . ." She paused, taking a long look at her fingernails in a casual show of confidence. "There must be some reason you're scared enough of children that you're trying to mind-control them all. But you're from the future. So maybe you know more than you're pretending?"

The masked man watched Elara carefully, clearly considering her words.

Elara stared back. "You know something about what happened last year at the Seven Systems School . . . Everyone does. About how the Frillianth tried to force their way into our reality. But do you know who the Frils are *really* afraid of? The person who is destined to defeat them, over and over?"

Elara pulled her collar tight, tugging at it with both hands.

"Yeah . . . ," she added. "I bet you do." Elara pulled the chrono-hopper out of her pocket. "And I bet you're interested to know where I got this."

"What you hold in your hands is impossible," the Watchman said. "You have no idea that device's capacity . . ."

Elara pressed a button, and the device activated. Several lights started blinking. She still didn't actually know how to make it do anything, but she had a strong feeling that it might not matter.

"I know one thing about this," she said, exuding confidence she did not possess. "It can open warp holes from one place to another. I'm also betting," she added as she stepped forward, "that you can lock on to its signal."

"So, come on . . ." She held the device high above her

head, pressing the button she knew would make the lights blink. "Come and get me. I dare you."

The Watchman held up his own chrono-hopper. "So be it," he whispered.

The air around Elara suddenly felt electric. The tiny hairs on her arm stood up. A wind blew through the deck of the ship, and she heard someone cry out in alarm. Then a portal opened up in front of her—a swirling vortex of energy.

She had seen this before—once. Back when Headmistress Nebulina was attempting to destroy Paragon, Groob had appeared in the sky through a similar-looking energy vortex.

But just as the thought crossed her mind, Elara's world faded to black. Elara was ripped through the fabric of space time, leaving the schoolship, and all her friends and allies, behind.

CHAPTER 017

When Elara woke up, she was in a very different place. The lighting was dim, with neon blues and reds pulsing from very powerful-looking computers. Most of the technology was recognizable—but not all of it.

Elara tried to sit up, but she was secured by two large straps. The gurney was being pushed by two robots, similar to those she had met on the schoolship. Long metal tendrils dragged from the bottom of each, serving as flexible limbs.

Realizing there wasn't much she could do at the moment, she took stock of herself. As far as she could tell, she had been left alone since she lost consciousness. She wasn't in any pain, she was in her usual clothes, and she even had her hip bag still attached to her belt.

She tapped her pocket and was comforted that it wasn't empty. She even still had the chrono-hopper. Evidently the robots didn't really think she was a threat and hadn't bothered to search her.

Just as they had planned.

But Elara's thoughts were soon interrupted by the familiar voice of the Watchman. "Bring her in," the time traveler whispered coldly.

The robots complied without hesitation, and Elara felt the gurney roll deeper into the room.

"The stolen schoolship has moved from the coordinates you procured," one of the robots offered. "The remaining students are still evading capture."

"It is possible they have taken refuge on the surface of a passing world—" the second robot added. "Or perhaps hidden themselves in a nebula—"

Elara could see the Watchman now. For the first time in the flesh. Well, sort of. He was covered head to toe in black, with his face hidden behind his mask.

The Watchman waved a commanding hand, and the

robot fell silent. "I do not care. This is the only student who matters. Continue to search for the rest, but do not disturb me unless they are found."

The two robots made agreeable buzzing noises, turned, and floated out of the room, leaving Elara alone with the villain who had complete control over the entire Galactic Affiliation.

"My apologies for the discomfort," the sinister Watchman said, pressing a button and releasing Elara from the bindings.

"Thanks," Elara grunted, rubbing her arms as she sat up.

"You know what I am," the Watchman said quietly. "How?"

"How?" Elara shrugged. "You don't know? I thought you were a time traveler. Shouldn't the present be, like, an open book to you?"

The Watchman ignored the question, instead reaching into his cloak and removing a familiar-looking device—his chrono-hopper. "Show me," he said. Elara instantly understood that this was not a request. Seeing no point in arguing, she reached into her pocket and removed her own chrono-hopper.

"Interesting," the Watchman whispered. He walked over and reached out, extending the chrono-hopper so that it almost touched the one Elara held. There was a spark of electricity arcing between the two devices. "Very interesting. These two devices . . . they are not just similar. They are the same."

The Watchman took a step back and pressed a button on a machine. A large mechanical arm with a laser at the end swung down from the ceiling. Elara decided to ignore the frightening-looking machinery as the masked figure continued his questions.

"That technology does not belong in this era. Where did you get it?" he said, tapping buttons as he spoke.

Elara shifted in place, angling her away from the Watchman.

"Where do you think?" she answered as she slowly opened the pouch of her hip satchel.

"You are associated with time travel in some manner—that much is clear."

"That's a way of putting it," Elara agreed. "So why are you doing this? I mean . . . I know what you are. But . . . why?"

As she spoke, Elara felt the expected movement of several small beings crawling out of her hip satchel, shielded from the Watchman by the angle of her body.

Everything was going according to plan.

"You are attempting to change the subject," the Watchman said, more agreeable than Elara expected. "But I see no problem in answering. You are clearly a being of special importance. You should understand what it is you struggle against."

He pressed a button. The scary laser on the mechanical arm flared to life. Elara glanced down toward the floor, just in time to see miniaturized versions of her friends slide down the leg of the gurney and run off behind a large control panel.

It had been a tricky and risky plan, and several of Elara's classmates had been against it. But Elara pressed the point: There was no way they could stand against the military forces of the Seven Systems. The schoolship was half-ruined and had no weapons and little in the way of defensive shielding. They were a floating target. Capture was inevitable. Elara argued that if they had to be captured, it was better to do so under their own terms. To let the bad guy think he had won while her friends, shrunken down using the scientific technology on board, sneaked into the Watchman's headquarters.

And it had worked . . . so far.

Elara glanced back up, relieved that the Watchman hadn't noticed anything. Then he threw a switch, and the laser ignited, shooting her directly in the head.

Elara felt like she should be screaming. It was a laser beam directly at her forehead, after all. But it didn't hurt. At least, not yet.

She glanced at the Watchman. The sinister masked figure was doing the last thing Elara had expected—removing his mask. With his gloved fingers, he tapped a series of locks on the edge of the mask, each one making a hissing noise as it released. Then he bent forward, pulling the mask slowly away from his face.

The Watchman looked up, his angry eyes staring directly at Elara. The young girl felt herself gasp in both shock and horror.

The Watchman was Agent Groob.

Then the laser beam intensified, and Elara felt her mind leave her body.

CHAPTER 018

Elara opened her eyes. She wasn't dead. That alone was a tremendous relief.

"Welcome to my world."

The voice belonged to the Watchman—though it wasn't muffled or synthesized through his mask. Elara looked around and caught sight of the evil time-traveling conqueror. He was standing on the edge of a cliff, looking down into an enormous valley. His black mask was off, held in his hand, which hung loosely at his hip.

"You clearly think I am nothing but an evil dictator," Groob whispered, his back still to Elara. "A warlord from the future, enslaving the past."

Elara was dumbfounded. She felt a rising sense of dread and panic. Whatever she had expected. . . . this was so very much worse. "I thought . . . ," she managed at last. "How can you be the Watchman?! Agent Groob . . . you saved me! You saved my school and the entire galaxy! How can you be evil now?!"

The Watchman gave a small laugh, his familiar face taking on an unfamiliar expression of cruelty.

"You speak of things I have never experienced. Of actions I would never take." He turned and looked at Elara, shrugging. "The man you met was not me."

"But . . . ," Elara scowled. "It's obviously you. I mean, you are Agent Groob, right? You look just like him."

"I am Tobiias Groob," the Watchman admitted. "But I am not the Tobiias Groob you know."

"But . . ." Elara stared, confused.

"Are you familiar with the concept of alternate realities?" Groob asked. "Of parallel universes?"

"You mean, like, in one universe you turn right, but in another universe you choose to turn left? Sort of . . . ?" Elara replied.

"It's more complicated than that, but you get the idea," the Watchman answered. "For every decision we make, for every choice, there is another reality where we chose the opposite. Each one locked away in its own quantum reality."

Groob waved his hand, and the galaxy started spinning. It was like they were fast-forwarding through the history of everything. Elara had to shield her eyes. It wasn't every day you got to see all of reality explode into existence around you.

"Your Groob was a time traveler, same as I am," the Watchman said. "From what I have been able to discern, he came back from his time, your future, and made changes. He altered his own time stream, and thus changed the conditions of his own, future existence."

"He helped us," Elara said quietly.

"And you have his chrono-hopper. So where is he now?"

Elara glanced away. "He's . . . gone, I guess? He appeared in my dorm, warned me that things were bad, then exploded into a bunch of light."

"Ah. As I expected," the evil version of Groob said with a sly smile. "He tampered with time. He changed things so that he would never exist, replacing him with me."

"But he's going to stop you . . . ," Elara said, struggling to stay positive.

"Child, I am sorry to tell you, but he is gone," the Watchman said, clearly not sorry. "He was erased from time. I am the only Groob now. And, I . . . I will not make the same mistakes that he did."

There was a long silence as Elara attempted to take in what she had just learned.

Her friend, Groob, was gone.

Elara shook her head, disoriented. "Where are we?" she asked. "Did you take me with you to the future?"

The evil Groob laughed. It was a sad tone. "No," he finally said. "There is no future for my world or for my people. What you see here . . . these are just memories. My memories."

Elara walked up to the edge of the cliff to stand next to the Watchman. For as far as the eye could see, metal and glass towers rose up from the ground, stacked one after another. There were no streets, just a series of transparent tubes filled with pod-like vehicles.

The city itself was enclosed in a bubble dome, and the sky above was pale green with pastel blue clouds.

"Wait . . . ," Elara said after taking it all in. "I know this planet. I've seen it in the holo-vids. This is Dulonia Prime." She glanced at Groob. "I didn't know you were Dulonian."

Groob laughed lightly to himself. "Ah . . . so your knowledge is not limitless. Regardless, I'm from Dulonia, though like you, my ancestry is primarily human."

Elara glanced out across the landscape again. "You said Dulonia Prime has no future. But it's one of the original Seven Systems. It's a capital planet along with Suparian Prime and Arcutiaa." She looked back at Groob, and he turned to look at her. For the first time she could really see his face. He was identical to the time traveler she had known, yet somehow completely different. His face was etched with deep sadness, while his eyes . . . his eyes said something else altogether.

"What happens to Dulonia?" Elara asked slowly. "There are billions of beings on this planet. What happens . . . to them?"

"Watch," was all Groob said.

And at that moment, a great explosion could be seen in the distance. It burned quickly across the sky, and Elara felt herself flinch.

"Calm yourself," the Watchman said. "It's just a memory."

The fire swept over them, and the city melted. The buildings were reduced to slag. The sky was filled with fire. Elara felt her eyes fill with tears. It was horrible. It was beyond imagining. And then it all stopped. The scene rewound. The fire retreated back to the point of the explosion. The buildings reformed. Everything was exactly as it had been.

“What . . . why did that happen . . . ?” Elara asked, overwhelmed with emotion.

“The moment replays in my mind,” the Watchman answered. “Over and over, just as it has since I witnessed it many, many years ago. The Frils, breaking free from their ancient temporal prison, burned my home world so that they might return.”

“But . . . but this hasn’t happened yet!” Elara cried. “Is that why you’re here? You’re going to stop this? Right? Is that why you’ve done all this stuff?”

“I will stop the Frils, yes,” the Watchman spoke, his voice tinged with fury. “I will ensure that they pay for their crimes. That they will never live to destroy the countless worlds they seek to consume.”

“And you’re going to save Dulonia?” Elara asked, seeking reassurance. “So . . . what you said before was wrong? Your planet *does* have a future, because you’re here to save it. Right?”

“No,” the Watchman placed his mask back on his face.

Elara felt herself grow cold. “What do you mean? All those people . . . your people—”

The Watchman turned and stared at her from behind his mask. Elara had seen a touch of it before in his eyes. Now she was sure of it.

The Watchman was insane.

“Dulonia must burn,” the masked figure responded.

"If it does not, I will not become the man I am. And if I am not this person you see before you, then who is it that will stop the Frils from destroying every civilized world? What happens to the rest of the galaxy if I stop everything to save my own people?"

"But you can stop the Frils from returning!" Elara countered.

The Watchman waved the argument away. "You speak out of ignorance. I have spent a lifetime examining this issue. The Frils will escape their prison, and my world will burn. So it is written, and so it shall be. But then . . . then I can stop them and save every other planet from the same fate. There is no other way. If I change events . . . then I would simply be erased like your own Groob was. And then who would keep the galaxy safe?!"

"I won't let you do that," Elara said, feeling slightly nauseous. "I won't let Dulonia die."

"As if I would leave you a choice," the Watchman hissed.

He stepped forward, looming over Elara. Elara stumbled backward, lifting an arm to shield herself. The Watchman raised his chrono-hopper and pointed it directly at Elara.

"And now you will— GUHH!"

Groob staggered, grasping at his head suddenly. Before Elara could even register what had happened, visions of Dulonia melted away. Suddenly she was back in the Watchman's lair. Evil Groob was on his knees, clutching his head. Nearby on the floor was a heavy-looking pipe. Elara shook her head, confused.

"Hey!" squeaked a tiny voice. "Get it together already! We gotta move!"

Elara looked down and saw her miniaturized friends on the floor in front of her. Knot, Beezle, Sabik, all jumping up and down trying to get her attention.

"Elara!" tiny Beezle said in her very tiny voice. "We must hurry! The evil bad person will not stay stunned for long!"

"Right . . . ," Elara said, still dizzy from the memory laser. "About that . . ." Elara pushed forward and shoved the mechanical arm so the laser pointed at Groob. Suddenly it was blasting his own memories back into his own head. The madman writhed and screamed in agony.

"Climb on!" Elara yelled, scooping up her little friends and placing them in her pocket before running through the facility. She had no idea where she was going, but anywhere was better than here.

"What did you find out?" she yelled to her friends inside her pocket.

"You were correct in your theories," Beezle yelled from the top of the pocket.

"They're using satellites. Lots of them, all broadcasting the same mind-control frequencies they use on the ships," Sabik added. "Every planet in the galactic core is under control!"

"It is horrible!" Knot growled. "The non-carbon-based life-forms . . . my people . . . they're immune. So instead, they're going to enslave them all with those nightmarish collars!"

"What about Clare?" Elara asked, rounding a corner. The satellite headquarters of the Watchman was massive, with lots of large rooms and twisted hallways.

"She's set, okay?" Sabik said with a shrug, answering Elara's question. "Don't worry about her. She knows what to do!"

Knot suddenly grew alarmed. "Look out!" she shouted, in her already high-pitched voice.

A robot flew out of the shadows. This one was larger than the ones on the schoolship. Its face screen displayed a simple expression of anger, while its tendrils arced with electricity. Two mechanical arms on either side of its red frame suggested that it was ready to attack.

The wall suddenly lit up—a massive floor-to-ceiling monitor. The screen immediately filled with the face of the Watchman. His eyes flared with rage, but when he spoke, it was with a voice that was cold and distant. “Eliminate her,” the robot said.

From Elara’s pocket, Beezle yelled, trying to offer encouragement. “It is just one robot, Elara!” The Arctuiaan was filled with her usual optimism. “You can defeat it, somehow. I believe in you!”

Then the robot’s hand began spinning with saw blades.

“Oh no! I was wrong!” Beezle yelled. “Run away with fastness!”

Elara backed up but quickly discovered the passage behind her had been locked—no doubt to cut off her escape. To her right was wall. To her left was wall.

“There’s nowhere to run!” Elara yelled to her friends.

“That is bad!” Beezle responded less than helpfully.

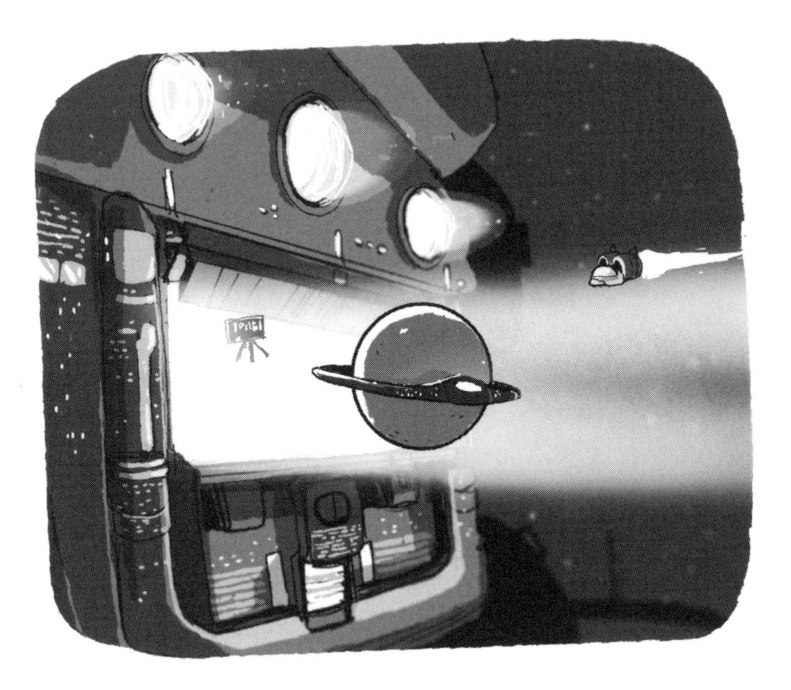

CHAPTER 019

"Ahhhh!" Elara yelled, ducking a saw blade.

The Watchman's voice rang out, speaking this time through the mouthpiece of the attacking robot. "I am sorry that it must be this way, Miss Vaughn, but you are an anomaly, and I cannot risk your interference."

An electrified tentacle grazed Elara's arm, zapping her with a violent shock.

"I represent peace!" the Watchman continued to

rant, growing louder and angrier with each word. “By my actions, a thousand worlds will live!”

A razor blade sliced the arm of Elara’s jacket, barely missing her skin. She tripped, and her shrunken friends tumbled out of her pocket, their tiny, squeaky screams drowned out by the voice of the Watchman.

“I will stop the Frils! No one will ever lose their planet as I did, no matter what the cost!”

There was nowhere to run. No place to hide. And there were way too many robots to fight, even if Knot had been full-size. Elara closed her eyes, waiting for the final strike. She hoped that, if nothing else, her shrunken friends might still escape.

Suddenly a loud crashing sound filled the air. The walls abruptly shattered into a hundred pieces and ruptured. Debris rained down, miraculously missing Elara and her friends. Elara blinked. It was a spaceship. A spaceship had crashed through the wall.

A hatch opened up, pouring light into the dark lair of the Watchman. Suue Damo’n stood at the hatch of the schoolship, sounding just as irritated as ever. “Well, hurry it up already!” she complained. “We don’t have all day!”

Elara scooped up her tiny friends and hurled herself into the open hatch, narrowly missing the electrified tentacles of the robots. Collapsing on the ship’s deck,

Elara turned and saw the hatch start to close behind her, just as more robots showed up, their hand blades spinning and their eyes glowing.

"Go!" Elara yelled. "Go! Go! GO!"

And then suddenly the ship tore free of the wall and blasted into space. Elara felt the deck of the ship tilt and the rough humming of the damaged engines through the rubberized flooring.

They had escaped. They were free. And more importantly, they had learned a whole lot about the Watchman.

Elara pulled herself up, checking on her friends. They were all a bit disoriented in her pocket, but no one was smooshed. "I am thinking," said the squeaky voice of Beezle, "that I am no longer enjoying the reduction of my size."

"If things are about to start getting better," Sabik muttered, "it will be worth it."

It only took a minute or two for Elara to reach the labs and use the miniaturization equipment to revert her friends to their proper size. A few seconds later and the group had traveled to the bridge. That's when things went from bad to worse.

The ship shuddered under Elara's feet. "What's happening?!" she yelled at Suue, who was sitting in the command chair.

"We're in the heart of the Seven Systems, and we flew a giant spaceship into the council satellite!" Suue snapped. "What do you think is happening?!"

Elara glanced at the screen, where several large and boxy government ships were moving in, surrounding the renegade schoolship. "There's too many of them," Elara heard herself whisper. "Jump to hyperspace!" she yelled louder.

"We can't yet! We don't have coordinates programmed!" Sabik shouted, pushing hard on the flight controls. The entire ship spun on its side, doing a complete 180-degree turn. Everything tilted, and Elara and Beezle tumbled across the deck in a painful somersault. Beezle slammed into a wall, while Elara grabbed one of the consoles, dangling from it by one hand.

"What are you doing?!" she yelled, her shoulder searing with pain.

"Flying at them!" Sabik yelled back.

Knot, who had managed to secure herself to a systems console, flipped a switch. "They're arming missiles!" the Grix yelled, an uncharacteristic edge of panic in her voice.

"Okay!" Elara yelled back.

"Well . . . what should we do?!" Knot said, frustrated.

"NOT GET SHOT!" Elara screamed.

The ship flipped around again, and once more Elara

and Beezle were both thrown toward the end of the command center.

"AAAH!" Elara shouted, slamming into one of the Milos. From a nearby station, Sapple reached out and pulled Elara into a free chair, helping her buckle in.

Beezle was upside down on the wall, which was where the floor would normally be. "What if we angle our shields to face the front of the ship?" Beezle suggested. "The ones designed to deflect space debris. They might also absorb the missile damage?"

"Yes!" Suue shouted. "Do that! Do that now!"

"Oh," Beezle said in a tone of deep sadness. "I meant that hypothetically. In all likelihood, it would take several days of mechanical engineering, not to mention software coding . . ."

"They're firing missiles!" Knot interrupted. "They're firing a lot of them!"

"Evasive maneuvers!" Elara yelled at Sabik through gritted teeth.

The surface of one of the boxy ships abruptly filled the monitor.

Sabik almost leaped out of the pilot's seat. "AAH!" he screamed. "TOO CLOSE! TOO CLOSE!"

"We're going to get hit!" Elara shouted.

Sabik tried to pull the ship up and was partially successful. The schoolship's bottom hull scraped along the council ship, taking out a radar dish and a chunk out of the schoolship. Alarms started shrieking loudly everywhere.

The hologram suddenly winked on, a blue flash filling the room. “Hello, students!” the headmistress said in an extremely chipper voice. “How can I be of assistance to—OH.” The hologram paused, taking a quick look. “Ohhh . . . Nope,” she said. “I’m out.” And with that, she blinked back off.

Elara looked at the readout in front of her. One of the large ships was launching triangular robot fighters. Lasers were blasting everywhere. The ship was venting oxygen.

“I’m jumping to hyperspace!” Elara said as the ship shuddered loudly.

Suue shook her head. “No! Sabik said it was too dangerous!”

“I was wrong!” Sabik yelled, now flying the ship with his eyes tightly shut, too afraid to look.

“Going to hyperspace!” Elara yelled, grabbing the lever and slamming it backward.

The ship did not go into hyperspace. In fact, the lever came off in Elara’s hand.

Knot shook her head. “Of course,” she said. “Of course this is what happens.”

“Stay calm!” Elara said, on the verge of panic.

"I just wanted to make planets with fluffy clouds," Knot continued. "Just fluffy clouds! Everyone else in my family wanted danger and violence! But me . . . 'I'll be a terraformer,' I said! Great job, past me!"

Elara slammed the hyperdrive console, trying to get it to work. "What about the missiles?" she shouted.

Knot shrugged. "They're about to hit us."

The missiles thudded into a section of the ship, ripping out one of the engines. The shrieking alarm began shrieking even louder.

Knot turned to look at Elara. "And then they hit us."

Suue looked like she was going to be sick. Knot was resigned to her fate. Sabik was literally flying blind. Sapple, Milo, and a few others were punching buttons on consoles just hoping for the best. But nothing was working.

"I don't want to interrupt the excitement," Beezle said from underneath the console. "But I believe everything will be okay now."

"You have a very strange idea of okay!" Sabik managed to say.

"No. Truthfully, things are okay," Beezle said with a smile. "Clare has succeeded in her mission. She has control of the Watchman's systems."

Sabik opened his eyes. Knot started examining readouts on his console. Sapple pushed a button.

"The council ships . . . ," she whispered in a papery thin voice, blinking her many eyes. "They're drifting? They're . . . they're completely offline!"

Knot gasped, excited. "We're not going to die!"

Suue mumbled, slumping in her chair. "Don't care. Just . . . please make the ship stop spinning . . ."

Sabik slowly brought the damaged ship to a halt. The last engine was sputtering but appeared to be operational. The hull breach had been sealed by helpful students quick to act.

Elara ran her fingers through her hair, shocked that the plan had worked. Clare never ceased to surprise her, time after time.

Clare was essentially a living, organic computer. Her ability to interface with machinery was vast, and the psychic connections that Beezle had managed to forge with the sponge magnified Clare's processing speeds.

In short . . . the largest weapon in the Watchman's army was offline. No more mind control anywhere in the Seven Systems.

But that wasn't the end. Not by a long shot. "Sabik, listen. For real," Elara said, "Can you get us out of here and to the Dulonia sector? Like . . . right now?"

Sabik squinted at Elara. "That's one of the original Seven Systems! There will be so many ships—"

"We need not worry much," Beezle reassured. "Clare

is quite clever, and we wired her into the Watchman's command center from a very remote location. We should encounter no significant resistance."

"But why there?" Knot pushed. "If we knocked out the mind control, the Watchman is basically beaten, right?"

Elara shook her head. "It's only temporary," she answered. "I mean, what happens if he fixes his Hypnoticon Broadcaster satellites somehow? We have to stop him completely. Forever. And there's only one way . . ."

Elara pressed a button, and the floor-to-ceiling monitor activated, showing a slowly rotating planet.

It was millions of miles away, but it was still there. Everyone was still alive. There was still time.

Elara dropped her voice down to a whisper. "We can do it," she said. "We can save Dulonia."

CHAPTER 020

According to Knot, who had been monitoring the communication channels, the fleet of the Watchman was in complete disarray. Some ships were even in open rebellion against the government, no doubt infuriated that a group of children was missing.

It meant that the path to Dulonia would be fairly clear. However, it would take the ship at least a day to reach the sector. Time that they didn't have. Luckily, there was another option on board the schoolship.

"Okay . . . ," Sabik said. "We're locked in for Dulonia. But what do we do once we get there? It's a big planet. Really big."

Sabik and Elara were on the bridge, as were Beezle, Knot, Suue, and both Milos. There were also several kittens running around and playing. They seemed to be quite adaptable to the ups and downs of the day, and none was injured from the recent battle.

"We have to stop the planet from blowing up," Elara answered, her confidence waning.

"Yeah," Sabik agreed. "But we don't even know what specific force blows the planet up. How are we supposed to stop it from happening?"

Elara waved away the concern. "It's a heavily populated planet," she said. "We'll find someone to help us—"

Knot was sitting in a corner of the bridge, at the sensor station, sipping tea. With that comment, though, she laughed so hard that she snorted tea out of her nostrils. "*Pff* . . . ," she said, tea dripping everywhere. "I am so sorry for the mess . . . but . . . no. Elara. Sweetie."

Elara felt her temper surge but remembered how difficult she had been at the start of this disastrous school year. Instead, she decided she would try to listen.

"Okay. Sorry, guys," Elara said. "I'm clearly not thinking it through. Help me understand why."

The young boy turned back as he walked. "Tobiias!" he called back. "Tobiias Groob!"

Elara's jaw dropped. She turned to her friends, then back to the little boy, watching him as he walked off and vanished around the bend. Finally, she just laughed.

"What is it?" asked a still-grumpy Knot as she pulled seaweed from behind her ear.

"Just time travel," Elara said. "It's really, really weird."

It took the better part of a day for the schoolship to show up. And it wasn't alone. A pair of massive Blossh star cruisers were running escort with it. After a few quick communications, the students were all brought on board one of the ships as respected guests.

Elara and her friends were the last to arrive, taking a shuttle up from the planet's surface. Together, they walked from the shuttle through the docking platform, finally arriving at the bridge—a section of the ship that appeared to serve as a throne room. The bridge was large, round, and coral-like. Many of the structures in the ship looked like they might have been grown from living reefs underwater. The atmosphere wasn't particularly pleasant, but it was breathable.

The doors slid open, and Elara was the first one

Knot finished dabbing her face with a napkin and poured another cup of tea. "Please, sit," she said in a very gentle voice.

Elara sat at the scanner station with the large Grix, while Knot poured a second cup of tea.

"You . . . ," Knot said, politely but firmly, "have the least experience of anyone on this ship with a capital planet. People aren't always comfortable with strangers. Especially ones running around warning about bombs."

"Plus," Sabik added, "we are on that 'wanted' list. Even if the Watchman is actually the bad guy, we still can't count on local authorities to not . . . y'know . . . arrest us."

Elara let out a deep breath. "Point taken," she said after a long moment of thinking. "Sorry. I just . . . I thought we had a solution."

Beezle stood up, looking thoughtful. "Elara . . . you have mentioned that the Watchman used some device to share his memories. Correct?"

"Uh . . . yeah," Elara answered. "While you guys installed Clare into the computer systems, he showed me the explosion on his home world."

"So, you have some idea of where you need to be," Beezle said confidently.

"Maybe?" Elara said, unconvinced. "I mean, it was a

city. But most of the planet is a city, right?"

"Seriously?" Suue sneered. "You didn't recognize which city? I mean . . . the skylines of Dulonia are famous—"

"Suue," Knot growled. "Have some tea."

"I don't really want—"

"Sit down," Knot said firmly, her voice heavy enough that it caused Elara's teeth to shake. "Sit and have some of this lovely tea and join us as we chat. Okay?"

Suue began to open her mouth but then thought better of it and sat down at the station with Elara and Knot. Knot produced a third cup and poured a cup of tea for the mean girl.

"I'm just . . . ," Suue started to say before changing course. "What I mean to say is . . . I agree with Knot," she said, finally. "Unless Elara has exact information, the exact location of the explosion could be anywhere. And she can't pinpoint it."

"But you know the cities of Dulonia well?" Beezle asked with curiosity.

"Yeah. My family owns some businesses there. And I'm from the Third Ring of Sahbrahntee. It's practically a neighboring system."

Beezle smiled. "Then you can help Elara identify the location! This is most helpful!"

Suue looked uncomfortable. "I mean . . . yeah?

But . . ." She glanced at Knot. "No offense intended, but it would take forever. And even then . . . she doesn't have much to go on. I need more info than what Elara can remember."

"Oh. I'm sorry," Beezle replied, smiling. "No . . . I did not mean you would discuss this with Elara. I meant I would link your minds, and you can share the memories directly and instantly."

"What?" Elara said, a look of horror on her face.

"You want me . . . ," Suue said, pointing at Elara, "to go into her head? Really?"

Elara gagged. "I think I'm going to be sick."

Suue glared at Elara. "It's not like I want to share memories with you!"

Knot poured more tea and politely cleared her throat. "Need I remind you, ladies, the fate of billions of lives hangs in the balance? Hmm?"

Suue sunk down in her chair, looking utterly defeated. "Ugggh," she said, diplomatically.

"Let's just get it over with." Elara glared.

"Excellent! You teamwork is admirable!" Beezle said with a clap. "Now, hold still. Normally, such a process would be very, VERY dangerous, but I believe, Elara, since your mindscape was recently manipulated, it should be possible—and likely not even painful?"

"Should be?" Elara asked, suddenly concerned.

"Likely?" Suue added.

Beezle offered up her most comforting smile. "Well. It would be no more painful than say . . . five hundred volts of electricity."

"That's . . ." Elara exchanged a glance with Suue. "That's . . . a lot. I mean . . . really a lot."

"Oh!" Beezle frowned. "Are your species electro-sensitive? Oh. I'm sorry."

"Why?" Elara asked, uncomfortable with where this was headed.

Beezle shrugged. "Because this will actually hurt quite a bit then."

And with that, the Arctuiaan placed her hands on the foreheads of the two girls, and everything went black.

Elara opened her eyes. She was back on her home planet, Vega Antilles V. Fields of grain stretched out as far as the eye could see. The silver light of the ringed moon was shining brightly, allowing a clear view across the landscape. Elara could even see her parents' farmhouse in the far distance. She could smell the damp grass under her feet. Everything was exactly as she remembered it, and she was suddenly overwhelmed with a sense of loneliness. She had just left . . . a week ago? But it seemed like years.

Elara knelt to the ground and scooped up a handful of the soft black soil that covered her farming planet. All terraformed, of course. Built by the Seven Systems to produce life-supporting grains. It was the perfect engineering that inspired her to pursue terraforming in the first place.

For a moment, none of it mattered. The Watchman. The threats of the Frils. Her mission. She closed her eyes and breathed in the air. For a moment . . . she was home.

"This place suuuucks," interrupted Suue Damo'n.

Elara rolled her eyes in exasperation. "Do you mind?" she asked impatiently.

"A little, yeah," Suue answered. "Like, kind of on a mission here. And this boring field—which I'm sure is precious to you in some absolutely boring way—is not Dulonia Prime."

"It's my home world," Elara answered defensively. "And this is how it looked the night before I left for school."

Elara heard a familiar voice. "Look!" her brother Danny yelled. "Check it out!"

Danny was running toward her, and Elara turned to greet her younger brother. She had barely thought of him since she was transported to the schoolship. How could she? Everything just kept . . . happening. She hadn't had any downtime since she left home.

And then Danny ran right through her, as if she weren't even there.

"Hello?" Suue said. "Just a memory? Remember?"

Elara turned and watched her brother run across the field, cutting a line through the grain as he moved. Her memory from a few weeks ago.

"Okay," Elara finally said, shaking her head. "So . . . we're in the wrong memory. How do we get to the right one?"

Instantly a door opened up in front of her. "Okay." Elara shrugged. "That was easier than I expected."

And then a second, identical door appeared.

"And now it just got harder," Elara said.

"How about this one? It feels right," Suue said, indicating the door on the left.

Elara glanced at it, then pointed to the one on the right. "I think we better go this way."

Elara reached out and opened the door, and suddenly everything turned upside down. They were somewhere else now. Somewhere familiar . . .

"Wait . . ." Suue squinted. "Is this the school train?"

Elara rubbed her eyes. It was the chain of shuttlecraft that had transported Elara to school her first year. "Why are we here?" Elara whispered to herself.

“Because you have a terrible sense of direction?” Suue asked.

“Shut up,” Elara answered as she pushed past the mean girl to explore the train.

“I remember this . . . ,” Elara said. “This was when I first walked the length of the train. It was . . . it was all so overwhelming and exciting. I had never seen so many different life-forms before . . .”

It was true. There were lots of humans and humanoids, but there were also fluffy yellow-and-green kids with gills, translucent crystalline students . . .

“Right,” Elara said to herself. “And the kid who looked like a living shadow. He ended up in one of my classes. Exo-biology, I think.”

Suue had walked a little bit ahead, but she suddenly stopped short. “Oh. Oh, I am so going to punch you when we get out of here,” Suue said, interrupting Elara’s trip down memory lane.

“What?” Elara responded, confused.

“Because I just discovered your first memory of me. And I hate you for it,” Suue said coldly.

Elara stepped forward. “Right. I was looking for a place to sit . . . and the first open seat I found was next to—”

“Buuhhh-duhhhh!” came an inarticulate voice from

one of the seats. "My name is Suue! And I like to eat used chewing gum! Faaaaarrt!"

Elara opened her mouth, then closed it again. It was, in fact, her first memory of Suue. Only it wasn't really Suue so much as a rude re-imagination of the mean girl.

"In my defense," Elara said with a voice tinged with shame, "you were pretty mean to me that first day. And the rest of last year, actually. So I may have misremembered things a tiny little bit."

The memory version of Suue managed to stick her entire hand up her own nose. "Woot!" she yelled. "I struck gold!"

The real Suue glared at Elara and stormed past. "Let's just find the way out of this memory," she grumbled as she pushed forward, shoving her way through another door.

Once again, everything flipped upside down and spun briefly, before Elara was able to focus on her new surroundings.

"Oh no . . . ," Elara moaned.

"Hey . . . I know this one," Suue said, looking around. "Visitors Day last year at STS. The day that Headmistress Nebulina tried to destroy the school."

"Yeah," Elara said, her voice grim. "Not my favorite day."

Suue looked out at the spectacle. "*Pff.* You seemed happy enough. Had an entire audience for your big dramatic moment!" Sure enough, the memories of Elara and the headmistress were at a standoff, with Headmistress Nebulina ready to use the terraforming bomb to transform the planet.

The explosion went off, and Elara looked away from the bright glare. It was Nebulina, consumed by her own weapon. Her atoms rearranged, her body burned away into salt before disintegrating completely. Elara looked up, expecting to see a memory of the good Groob burst forward to save the day.

Instead, the Watchman floated above—or at least a mental construct of him did.

"Elara . . . ?" Suue said, sounding uncertain. "What's wrong . . . ?"

"I can see the Watchman . . . the evil Groob," Elara said, feeling overwhelmed. "He's . . . it's like he's in my memory. In a place he shouldn't be."

"Then we're probably getting close, right? I mean . . . if you're seeing him here—"

"I think . . . ," Elara said, reaching up, "I think maybe . . . he's trying to intimidate me. Scare me away from the memories."

Suue shrugged. "How can he do that? We're in your memory, not his."

"I don't know," Elara answered. "I've never done any of this before."

Suue looked around. Everything was transforming into a hurricane of energy. "Whatever we're doing here . . . maybe hurry it up? I think we need to leave, now."

Elara pushed forward. The false memory of the Watchman looked down at her and sneered. Instantly Elara felt her head start to pound again. The energy inside her pressed forward . . . wanting release. She hadn't been able to control it. She hadn't been able to make her power work on command. But now. . . .

She extended her glowing hands toward the false Watchman. It exploded out of existence.

"That. Was cool," Suue murmured under her breath.

Suddenly everything flipped around and spun again. The false version of the memory had been erased, and with it, Dulonia suddenly came into view.

Elara opened her eyes and looked out across the horizon. She and Suue had finally arrived at the right city, at the right moment in time. The Watchman's past. Elara's present. Dulonia stretched out in front of the pair. But it was . . .

"Burning," Suue said.

CHAPTER 021

"The core of the planet?" Sabik asked, incredulous. "How are we supposed to stop that?"

"I don't know . . . ," Elara responded, feeling lost. "I mean . . . I thought it would be like last year, with terraforming bombs."

Elara and Suue had returned from their trip inside Elara's head and had recovered from their journey. The two girls felt more or less okay, though Elara's head was pounding from the confusing ordeal. Now they were resting on the ship's bridge, seated at the various computer stations and terminals.

Knot ground her large stone hands together, nervous. "Do we have enough time to stop Dulonia from exploding? Or maybe warn someone?" the Grix said.

Suue shook her head. "According to the Watchman's memories, the planet's core will detonate in less than an hour. Then the terraforming energy will sweep across the planet, converting everything—every blade of grass, every building, every person—into raw energy. The resulting explosion will be powerful enough to unlock the time stream and help the Frils escape from their prison."

"Acid neutralizes the chemical reaction . . . ," Elara pushed. "Maybe we can insert a compound into the planet's core?"

Beezle shook her head. "There is no such acid that could survive that. Anything would boil away instantly."

"Besides . . . ," Suue added. "It would just add more pressure to the planet core. Even if you stop the energy wave, the chain reaction would probably blow the world up."

Elara blinked, slowly standing up. "Wait . . . blowing up the planet. That could work."

Beezle quickly shook her head. "Oh! No, Elara . . . Blowing up planets is very bad! That is what we are trying to stop! Was your brain maybe damaged by the mind link?"

Elara shook her head. "No, seriously . . . listen. If there is an atomic reaction of terraforming energy inside the planet's core, we might be able to stop it by venting the excess pressure off into space!"

Sabik looked at Elara like she had grown an extra set of eyes. "You mean like . . . volcanoes?" The Suparian shook his head.

"It's Terraforming 101!" Elara said with growing excitement. "If we vent the pressure of the planet core, we can interrupt the process before it can really start to build! And any contaminated matter we could purge in the process!"

"In theory . . . ," Beezle considered. "In theory, it could work. But the process would damage the world severely. I do not think this is a viable solution."

Elara felt frustrated, but rather than argue she sat back down. "Okay. Okay, maybe that's true. But . . ."

She paused, gathering her thoughts, thinking back to the previous school year. Back then, she had discovered that a series of waves could stop rapid terraforming energy. A "wave packet" it was called. One could theoretically stop an energy cascade with a second cascade—like when two waves hit each other in the water, they cancel each other out.

Elara quickly began typing at the computer terminal, ideas buzzing in her head. "Does Dulonia have a magnetic core?"

Suue furrowed her brow, thinking. "I believe so. I mean . . . yeah. I remember reading about that back when I visited the capital—"

"Got it," Elara interrupted as she continued to type. After a moment, the large floor-to-ceiling monitor began displaying a series of wavelengths. "Look," Elara said excitedly. "We don't need to physically destabilize the chemical process. The chemicals are just a catalyst. We need to stop the energy reaction—and we can do that by creating a nullifying wave!"

"Aah . . . ," Beezle said, "that is very interesting. The energy wave we generate would be the opposite frequency of the destructive terraforming wave!"

"Yes!" Elara said, typing some more. The monitors shifted, showing Dulonia Prime on the screen. Three red lights appeared at different positions on the globe, all connecting to create a triangle. "See!" Elara exclaimed, getting more and more excited. "The planet of Dulonia Prime has three poles rather than the standard two—which actually helps us create a comprehensive net of wavelengths."

"An electromagnetic pulse generator—like the one I used to take out the ship," Suue said, seeing where Elara was going. "But the planet . . . I mean, that could be more destructive than the terraforming bomb!"

"Right!" Elara agreed. "Except this will occur inside the planet core! It will erase the terraforming bomb wave! The two will cancel each other out completely! No one on the planet would ever even know it happened!"

"So, we just have to set up broadcast terminals." Sabik scratched his chin. "A lot easier than volcanoes."

"And a lot less destructive," Suue agreed. "It's . . . a plan, anyway."

"We have transmitters on board," Knot added. "Lots of them. It wouldn't take long to adapt them to create a portable broadcast . . . but we will need an energy source to power the wave."

Elara pulled out the chrono-hopper. "I can handle that."

Knot furrowed her brow. "And you know how to use that thing now?"

"Only a little," Elara admitted. "But I was in the Watchman's mind. I think I managed to pick up a few things he didn't mean for me to see."

Elara punched a few more buttons on the console. The screen showed three points of cascading energy flowing toward the planet's core, meeting in the center, then bouncing backward. "See . . . ," she continued. "As long as we make sure all three transmitters are linked, I can just power the whole thing wirelessly from one of the locations."

"And this will save the planet . . . today?" Suue asked, still skeptical. "What's to stop the Watchman from doing it all over again?"

Elara shook her head. "The Watchman told me himself. He became who he is after seeing his world destroyed. But if that never happens . . . ," Elara said, cracking her knuckles together. For the first time in a long time, she had the feeling that things might really be getting better. That there might be hope.

The ship was in distant orbit of Dulonia. Close enough to launch the scary transport tubes, while just out of range for anyone to detect the ship as a threat. In the hangar, Elara stood in one transport tube, ready to launch. Nearby, Suue and Sabik stood inside another, while Beezle and Knot were waiting in a third. There was a large console controlling all the tubes, with Sapple and Xavie monitoring.

Elara and the two groups preparing to transport each held a large pole—roughly seven feet in length. All three poles had radar dishes attached, as well as a fair amount of wiring and electric bits that had been hastily cobbled together.

"We plugged in the coordinates," Sapple said, looking very uncomfortable. "But . . ."

"This is a terrible idea," Xavie added. "No one on board really knows how to use this stuff."

"So there's a super-strong chance you're just going to squish into the surface of the planet," Sapple continued.

Elara shrugged, trying to hide her nervousness. "Hey, if we stuck to only doing what we knew how to do, the universe would be a very, very boring place."

Beezle looked uncharacteristically frowny. "I supplied you the manual. You did read it, correct?"

Xavie looked apologetic. "It's over two hundred thousand pages long. You gave it to me, like, ten minutes ago. So . . . I did not."

"Oh," Beezle said. "Oh no."

"Activating!" Sapple yelled, throwing a large and impressive-looking lever. "Everyone hold on to your molecules."

The tubes rocketed out of the spaceship at an impossibly fast speed. Elara felt every atom of her body start to shake. She had closed her eyes instinctively but managed to open them for a brief second to see the surface of the planet coming up at her tiny metal space tube superfast. "Why . . . ?" she whispered to herself. "Why would anyone think it was a good idea to travel like this?"

She closed her eyes and waited to either land or turn into a smudge on the surface of the world below.

She did not turn into a smudge.

Elara carefully lifted her face up out of the mud. The transport tube had been . . . rougher than her previous journey. And she had to take a very long minute to catch her breath.

The first thing Elara noticed was the sky—a green sky with pastel blue clouds. She stood up and finally staggered to the top of a hill. A hill, which likely meant a view. She could get her bearings . . .

. . . though she was pretty certain she knew what she would see.

And she was not disappointed. A massive bubble city, sitting nestled in a distant valley.

It looked exactly like Elara had seen in the Watchman's memories. Even the clouds were in the same positions.

Suddenly Elara remembered her mission. There was no time to wait. The explosion could happen any second. Elara risked a quick look at the time. It had been almost ten minutes since she had arrived.

Hopefully, her friends had gotten their antennae locked in place.

Elara slammed her antenna into the ground as deeply as it would go. Quickly unraveling the coiled wires, she stretched them out and anchored them to the ground as well. These would help stabilize the frequency of the wavelength—hopefully.

Elara glanced at the sky. Not long . . . not long at all. She hit the button on her communicator. She wouldn't be able to reach the ship—it was too far away. But the two teams were on the planet, even if they were all on opposite hemispheres.

"Beezle? Knot?" she called. She waited a moment. Static. "Sabik? Suue? Anyone there?"

Nothing.

Elara began to panic. And then her breath escaped her as she heard the sound of a familiar laugh . . .

The Watchman was here.

"How . . . ?" Elara started to ask.

"What is there to stop me from coming here, Elara? You of all people know I am not bound by space or time!" He flicked his wrist, flourishing the chrono-hopper in his hand. It buzzed and emitted a green light.

"I'm going to save this planet!" Elara protested loudly, positioning herself between the Watchman and the antenna.

"Elara . . ." The evil version of Groob sighed loudly. "Could you possibly be more heroic? Rocketing yourself across the galaxy to a doomed planet with nothing but some metal sticks to save you?"

Suddenly her comm system shot out a burst of static. It was Knot—though the interference made it difficult to hear. "We're"— *zzzt*—"position . . . ," Elara heard her friend shout. "Sabik says"—*zzzt*—"ready, too!"

Elara pulled the chrono-hopper from her jacket pocket, staring directly at the Watchman, waiting for him to make some kind of move.

"I'm sorry," Elara said, the softness in her voice quite real. "I know that saving your world will mean that you'll never exist. But no matter how many you think you're saving by letting your world die . . . it's not worth the price. The Frils will be stopped. Just like before."

Elara pressed the button on the chrono-hopper, and a charge of electricity poured out of it and into the antenna. The makeshift wave generator glowed with power, the sensor lights attached to the side all igniting with crimson symbols, broadcasting to the two sister devices across the globe. The radar dish turned and slid downward, as it was designed to do, locking into place. The lights all turned blue, and the wave began to broadcast.

It was done. The wavelength would interfere with the atomic conversion cascade. The Frils wouldn't be freed. The planet would survive.

"I imagine that you're probably congratulating yourself?" the Watchman asked, his smile locked in place.

Elara blinked and looked around. "You're still here?" she asked with dawning horror. "How can you still be here? The wavelength. . . . should work." A sense of dread kicked in. "They have to work," she whispered.

The evil version of Groob laughed. "They will work amazingly well," he answered. "More perfectly than you might have imagined. You are quite brilliant, Miss Vaughn. Have no doubt of that."

"Then . . . ," she stammered uncertainly, " . . . then how can you still be here?"

"I was like a professor to you in that other reality. That other version of me? Correct?" The Watchman smiled. "Then I want you to think carefully. You are attempting to stop an explosion at the heart of the planet with energy waves." The evil time traveler leaned in, his smile widening. "Who was it then, who told you there was a terraforming bomb at the heart of this world?"

Elara's brow creased. "It was . . . you. I accessed your memories. When you shared your memories with me . . . I . . . I went back in and looked deeper . . ."

"And saw what?" The Watchman tapped the side of his head with one finger. "You only saw what I wanted you to see, my dear girl."

Elara felt the ground shake. She looked around frantically, trying to think. The wave she had just broadcast into the center of the planet. It was meant to cancel out the opposing wavelength from the terraforming bomb. But . . .

"There is no terraforming bomb," Elara said, her voice hoarse and thin. "There never was a bomb. Your world. Dulonia Prime is destroyed by . . . oh no . . . no . . ."

Groob looked out across the horizon, a touch of sadness in his mad eyes. "By three wavelength generators, all firing at once, projected into the heart of the planet. Oh yes."

"The destroyer of my world, Elara Adele Vaughn, is you. It has always been you."

CHAPTER 022

Elara staggered backward, reaching for her comm device. "Wait!" she called out. "Turn everything off! Knot? Beezle? Anyone . . . turn them OFF!"

"It's too late for that," the Watchman said, shaking his head in mock sadness. "The chain reaction has already started, deep within the core."

Elara felt time slow down. She could feel the earth shaking beneath her feet. She could hear the deep rumbling sounds emanating from far below the surface. She knew she had only one chance. Only a fraction of a second to act, and then maybe . . . maybe she could stop the process she had started. Maybe she could save the planet.

The Watchman laughed. "You cannot escape!" his voice rang out. "I come from the future! I know what will happen! What has already happened! This is your end. This is the end of your friends. This is the end of—"

And then Elara socked the evil time-traveling dictator in his face.

"Urk!" the Watchman said, sputtering. "You . . . wha?!"

Elara socked him again. "You are a very, VERY bad person!" she yelled. "There is nothing of the Groob I knew in you. NOTHING!"

"But you can't—" he started to reply, but Elara hit him again, knocking him out. Her skin was burning. Her heart was racing. Every cell in her body felt like it was going to erupt. But this time . . . this time Elara knew what to do with it.

"No! That's not how it happens . . . ," the evil version of Groob managed to sputter, semiconscious.

"You're a time traveler, Groob," Elara said as she picked up his chrono-hopper. "You of all people should know . . . we can change the timeline. And that's what I'm going to do!"

Elara's comm buzzed. It was Sabik. "Elara!" she heard him yell. "What's happening! Everything's starting to shake!"

Elara adjusted the chrono-hopper. She hoped she had guessed the controls correctly. If not . . . "It's okay," she said. "I have a plan."

Elara heard Suue cut in. "A plan!" she heard the mean girl shout. "We had a plan, and it's not working! What are you talking about?!"

Elara shrugged. "I'm going to teleport into the planet core," she answered. "Tell everyone . . . tell everyone bye. And that I'm sorry."

"WHAT?!" Suue shrieked loudly enough to cause the comm speaker to hiss. "Whatever you're up to, don't—"

Elara turned a dial on the chrono-hopper. She closed her eyes and pressed a button and with a flourish waved the device in the air.

And vanished.

Elara materialized exactly where she intended to. She was buried right in the liquid heart of the planet. Engulfed in pure magma.

Ow, she thought. *That is seriously hot.*

It was. It really was. It was hotter than anything the young girl could have ever imagined. It was, Elara guessed, not unlike taking a vacation on the surface of an exploding sun, or maybe a quick dive into a swimming pool filled with liquid laser beams.

Super, super hot.

But Elara wasn't actually burning.

Instead, every pore of Elara's body was radiating pure atomic energy. The terraforming power that had been churning inside her ever since she swallowed the marble was pouring out now. And not just in a quick explosive burst, but in a constant pulse of rhythmic waves. Consequently, the heat was reaching Elara but not burning her.

Elara looked on in awe as the magma surrounding her was slowly transformed. Boiling molten rock turned into water and then into steam and then into dry earth and grass. The wave of transforming energy was building, altering each layer of atoms. Already, there were several feet of space around Elara. She was floating in the air above a grassy outcropping.

Elara flexed, and even more energy burst from her, saturating the space around her. She felt alive. Strong. Empowered. Everything she touched would change, and she could see it happening. She could see each atom rearranging itself. Even more, she could reach out with her mind. Push the atoms. Tell them what she wanted. Direct their change.

Elara looked at her hands, then stretched them out, feeling power exploding from each fingertip. It was incredible, and she never, ever wanted the feeling to stop. The energy was pure and clean and wonderful.

Feeling the resistance of the two wavelengths collide, she relaxed, pulling back the power that wanted to escape from within. She could feel it: The planet core was now stabilizing itself.

It was over.

Feeling the magma start to push back against the bubble she had created, Elara quickly pressed a button on the chrono-hopper. She hoped very much it was the right one.

It was. After a quick cortex-like burst of energy, she vanished, just before the magma collapsed back into place, filling the gap where she had stood.

CHAPTER 023

Elara was able to use the chrono-hopper to reach Sabik and Suue quickly. The pair had landed in the heart of a major downtown area and were on the verge of being arrested when Elara warped into place, deactivated the antenna, grabbed them, and warped back out.

It was a bit worse for Beezle and Knot, whose coordinates ended up being on a small island bombarded by giant waves. The pair were miserable and drenched and overall unhappy. Regardless, they had managed to keep their antenna functioning, despite being attacked by gargantuan monsters.

With one last twist of the chrono-hopper, the group of students warped back to where Elara had left the Watchman.

Evil Groob was there, but he wasn't well. His reality had been erased. And soon he would cease to exist.

"You have . . . no idea . . . ," the withered husk of the evil time traveler hissed. "What you have done."

"We saved a planet," Elara responded, beaming. "We also stopped you and all your mind-control goons. The galaxy can go back to what it's supposed to be. So . . . yeah," Elara said, smiling, "I think we know what we've done."

"I was . . . going to make you safer . . . ," he gasped as he faded. "All of you . . . the entire galaxy stronger, safer!"

Elara frowned, her voice heavy and sad. "But would it be worth it?" she asked, already knowing the answer.

And then the Watchman was gone. Erased from existence.

Suddenly Elara caught sight of something moving. Just on the other side of the hill, a small figure was watching them. Elara moved hesitantly toward the being, wondering what new threat had materialized now.

There was no threat. Instead, it was just a small child—a young boy with dark skin and closely cropped hair. He looked very nervous and started to move back when Elara approached him.

"Who are you?" the boy asked.

"My name's Elara," she answered. "Elara Adele Vaughn." She pointed to her friends who were still some distance away, talking among themselves. "That's Sabik, and Knot, and Beezle. The other one is Suue."

"Oh," the boy said. "Why did that man you were talking to disappear?"

"He was a bad guy," Elara explained. "He was trying . . . Well, it doesn't matter. Don't worry. You're safe. No one's going to hurt you."

The boy seemed to think about that for a short moment, then nodded. "Okay," he responded. "I guess I should go home. I saw all sorts of flashy lights and heard yelling, so I thought something cool was happening." He looked around and shrugged. "I guess not."

Elara smiled. "Yeah, I think everything is settling down now."

With that, the boy turned and started to walk away. Elara paused for a second, then called out, "Hey, kid. What's your name?"

through. What she saw caught her so off guard that she stopped dead in her tracks. "Is that . . . ," she stammered. "Is that Clare?" she finally whispered, in awe.

It was. And she wasn't just leaning against a wall this time. No. Now the rectangular yellow sponge was leaning against a throne, decorated with a crimson-and-gold sash as well as a heavy, wide crown designed to fit her flat, cornered top area.

Beezle smiled and stepped forward, slowly rotating. "Oh, Clare, your species makes such wonderful spaceships! It is so exciting that you rushed to come and rescue us!"

"But why is she wearing a crown?" Elara asked, confused.

"I told you!" Sabik said. "Her full name is Clare Von Valentinus! She's heir to the Von Valentinus empire. She's owns her own star system!"

"Sure," Knot said. "But how is she here? Last time we saw her she was shrunk to a tiny size and was on the satellite headquarters of the Watchman!"

Beezle walked forward and placed her hand on Clare's yellow surface. "Ah. It seems our friend has had many bold adventures," Beezle said, speaking with closed eyes as she concentrated on the link she shared with Clare. "She narrowly escaped detection on the satellite after sabotaging the mind-control computer system."

Beezle focused, concentrating for a minute before continuing. "Evidently, she battled an entire squadron of the robots from the future and even cast down a major lieutenant during a life-or-death struggle above the satellite's nuclear reactor. This was after she managed to cobble together the technology needed to reengage her to proper size."

"Wait, what?" Elara asked.

"Yes," Beezle said. "She has had quite an epic adventure. Her people are apparently writing ballads about it as we speak."

Elara looked around. There were several other Blossh on board. Red, green, orange, blue. Some were cubes. Some were orbs. But all of them were completely immobile. Clare, for her part, continued to simply lean in place, saying and doing nothing, just like always.

Eventually, Elara and her friends were brought up to speed. Unable to be properly controlled by the Watchman's future tech, the Blossh were ready to strike as soon as the spell was broken on the rest of the fleet. Over the course of the last day, more than 90 percent of the Seven Systems Galactic Affiliation had been liberated, and with the reversion of the timeline, the remaining robots from the future had deactivated and self-destructed.

After a day of rest and recuperation, the students

of the schoolship were all curious about their future. It seemed that the newly reformed council had determined that the best place for students was back in school—the proper school this time. And as such, they would all be delivered to the newly remodeled and reopened Seven Systems School of Terraforming Sciences and Arts, where they would finish out the school year.

Elara and her friends returned to the battered schoolship that had been their home. In a weird way, Elara realized, she would miss the place. And she said as much to Beezle.

"Oh, do not worry!" Beezle said cheerfully. "I have prepared for you a gift so that a part of this place shall always be yours!"

The Arctuiaan handed Elara a portable projection. This one had clearly been modified, though. "What . . . what is it?" Elara asked.

With a blue flash of light, the machine came to life. "Hello!" shouted the still poorly rendered holographic headmistress. "I have prepared for you a poem!" The headmistress then placed her holographic hand under her holographic armpit and began making horribly rude noises.

"Oh," Elara said, her smile frozen in place. "So . . . thoughtful. Yay."

As they packed up their belongings for the transfer back to Paragon, Elara thought hard about a few things she needed to say to her friends.

"Hey . . . ," she started, feeling uncomfortable. "I just wanted to say . . . I am sorry that I kind of, you know, got bossy this last week. After last year . . . and then feeling like no one was really listening . . ."

Knot shrugged. "Don't worry about it. I mean, it's not like you were wrong. There was a time-traveling, mind-controlling tyrant trying to take over the galaxy."

"It has all worked out for the best," Beezle said, smiling.

Sabik was more distracted. "I don't understand, though," the Suparian pushed. "I mean, if all this happened because of the evil version of Groob, then why isn't it all erasing like he did?"

An explosion of light interrupted Sabik, and everyone turned to see a vortex opening up inside the room. "Nope. No more crazy stuff," Suue said, rolling her eyes. And with that, the mean girl walked out of the room.

A figure emerged from the vortex, his features hidden by the blinding light until the very last moment. All four students were on guard, ready to fight whatever it was. Even the tiny kitten creature Mister Floofyface was ready to launch himself at whatever came through.

"Relax," the figure said. "I come in peace."

"Groob?" Elara whispered as she saw the time traveler's face. "Is it you . . . or . . . ?"

Agent Groob smiled. "It's me. I'm back. Thanks to all of you. You repaired the damage my interference did to the time stream. Everything is as it should have always been."

"No offense," Sabik said, "but you know you look just like the guy who was trying to blow us all up. So . . . how do we know?"

"Sabik," Groob answered, looking directly at the Suparian. "In the future you will be renowned as an author—though your inability to master the art of grammar will lead to you enduring a series of harsh reviews. The resulting stress will cause you to lose your hair, a blow from which your fragile ego never quite recovers."

"Oh yeah, it's him," Sabik muttered. "I forgot . . . I forgot how fun he was," he added sarcastically.

"Agent . . . ?" Beezle asked. "Why hasn't everything snapped back to as it was?"

"Temporal misalignment," Groob answered. "Same reason you all didn't forget about me or the things I did after I was erased from reality. My future no longer existed because of things I did in my past. Which is a paradox, and the universe hates paradoxes—"

"I hate time travel," Knot moaned.

"It is fairly ridiculous," Groob agreed.

"What about me?" Elara interrupted. "Groob . . . what did you do to me?"

There was a long silence as the agent sighed. "Elara," he said. "I didn't do anything. Not really."

"But that energy . . . ," Elara pushed back. "It was the energy from the terraforming bombs. But somehow . . . I'm generating it now."

"You swallowed that marble last year," Groob explained. "You saved everyone that day, Elara. But you didn't walk away unchanged. This power . . . this will always be a part of you now."

Elara felt tears sting her eyes, but she refused to let them fall. "But I can't control it," she said. "I couldn't stop using it. It was . . . it was scary."

"My chrono-hopper?" Groob asked.

She handed the device to the time traveler. He fiddled with a few dials, then pointed it at her. Elara winced, afraid it would trigger some kind of reaction. But nothing happened.

"I'm just scanning you," he said reassuringly. "The energy is locked away. Mostly."

"This guy just loves his riddles," Sabik said dryly.

"Your body has to be in great danger to provoke a reaction," the agent continued. "You have to know, for certain, that your life is about to end. Otherwise, it's held back."

"By what?" Elara asked.

"By you. By your subconscious mind." The agent kneeled and gripped Elara by both shoulders. "It will be hard. Sometimes very hard. But you can tame this. I promise you."

"You're not . . . you're not going to help me?" Elara asked, confused.

"I'm sorry. I wish I could, but . . . I've damaged the time stream too much already. If I stay . . ." He sighed. "If I stay, something much worse than the Watchman could happen. I'm sorry. I have to leave you to your own devices now."

Groob flicked his chrono-hopper. A flash of light erupted, and a portal opened behind him.

"Be strong, Elara Adele Vaughn," Groob said, saluting. "All of you be strong, and stay together."

"And beware the Frils," he said ominously as he vanished.

EPILOGUE

A hooded figure stood amid the ruins of a long-dead world. Scattered across the landscape were statues, long fallen, the faces pounded by the sands of time.

The figure reached inside the pouch it was carrying. Inside were marbles—each one carefully crafted. Each one unique.

“Beware . . . ,” hissed the hooded figure. “Beware the empire that did not care.”

A long, clawed hand dropped a marble to the

ground. Where it landed, the ground started turning black. "They were lost," the hooded figure continued. "Lost, and their spirits do roam."

The blackness swelled like a bubble. Then it receded. The land below was no longer empty. Instead, on the ground was a massive egg, sickly and translucent green in color. Inside, something moved.

The figure pulled back its hood. The woman's face was lean and catlike, though it had suffered many wound and scars. Her teeth were long and jagged, and one of her ears was missing. And her eyes . . . her eyes were wild. Her eyes shone with madness.

"In search . . . ," she continued, "of a new, eternal home."

With that, Nebulina, former headmistress of the Seven Systems School of Terraforming Sciences and Arts, pulled out another marble from her pouch and began to repeat the incantation.

LANDRY Q. WALKER has been making stories happen for over twenty years. His work includes Star Wars novellas, a *New York Times* best-selling collaboration with Dean Koontz called *House of Odd*, the beloved comic book series *Supergirl: Cosmic Adventures in the 8th Grade* for DC Comics, the novella *Frozen: Phantoms of Arendelle* for Disney, and the celebrated superhero epic *Danger Club*. With his frequent collaborator Eric Jones, he also created the comic book *Little Gloomy*, which now airs internationally as the animated TV show *Scary Larry*.

KEITH ZOO is an illustrator living in Boston, Massachusetts. For the past decade, he's been the Lead Artist at FableVision Studios, working on a full range of things from character design and animation layout, to interactives and design. When he's not doodling monsters, goblins, and other silly things, he's spending time with his wife and daughter. To check out more of Keith's work, head on over to keithzoo.com.